THE
BAREFOOT
GIRL

THE
BAREFOOT
GIRL

A Novel of St. Margaret

CATHERINE MONROE

 NEW AMERICAN LIBRARY

New American Library
Published by New American Library, a division of
Penguin Group (USA) Inc., 375 Hudson Street,
New York, New York 10014, USA
Penguin Group (Canada), 90 Eglinton Avenue East, Suite 700, Toronto,
Ontario M4P 2Y3, Canada (a division of Pearson Penguin Canada Inc.)
Penguin Books Ltd., 80 Strand, London WC2R 0RL, England
Penguin Ireland, 25 St. Stephen's Green, Dublin 2, Ireland (a division of Penguin Books Ltd.)
Penguin Group (Australia), 250 Camberwell Road, Camberwell, Victoria 3124,
Australia (a division of Pearson Australia Group Pty. Ltd.)
Penguin Books India Pvt. Ltd., 11 Community Centre,
Panchsheel Park, New Delhi - 110 017, India
Penguin Group (NZ), cnr Airborne and Rosedale Roads, Albany,
Auckland 1310, New Zealand (a division of Pearson New Zealand Ltd.)
Penguin Books (South Africa) (Pty.) Ltd., 24 Sturdee Avenue,
Rosebank, Johannesburg 2196, South Africa

Penguin Books Ltd., Registered Offices: 80 Strand, London WC2R 0RL, England

First published by New American Library, a division of Penguin Group (USA) Inc.

First Printing, April 2006
10   9   8   7   6   5   4   3   2   1

NEW AMERICAN LIBRARY and logo are trademarks of Penguin Group (USA) Inc.

LIBRARY OF CONGRESS CATALOGING-IN-PUBLICATION DATA:
Monroe, Catherine.
The barefoot girl: a novel of St. Margaret / Catherine Monroe.
p. cm.
ISBN 0-451-21771-3 (trade pbk.)
1. Margaret the Barefooted, St., d. 1395 2. Italy—History—1268–1492—Fiction.
3. Abused wives—Fiction. I. Title.
PS3613.O5367B37 2006   2006
813'.6—dc22   2005027376

Set in Giovanni   Printed in the United States of America

For Tim and Kristen

THE
BAREFOOT
GIRL

Chapter 1

I<small>F</small> G<small>OD</small> <small>OR</small> S<small>ATAN</small> had not willed it differently, I would have remembered the day as the one on which I gave up my maidenhead to Augustino. As it happened, my virginity was not all that was sacrificed that summer day in the year of Our Lord 1340, when I was fifteen. A contract was drawn up between my father and a certain gentleman that meant I had to give up all that I held dear.

I am Margherita of San Severino, known as the Barefooted One, an old woman now, and I will tell you this story in the best way I can, but you must understand that it is another who writes it down for me, since I am not a learned woman. My words will not be woven together in the way that will make a rich tapestry, soft to your senses. It will be a rough swath of a story as coarse and unadorned as my beginnings, smelling of the earth and sweat and blood and tears and all the secretions of humanity. It is my confession, my prayer for atonement.

I was not to know about the contract for several days, although I did see the gentleman as he approached the wheatfield where my sister and I worked behind our father, helping him with the harvest. The land is fertile on the March of Ancona,

1

and if the rains fall right, as they had recently, the harvest is bountiful. It is hard work, harvesting, because we women who walked behind the men with the sickle had to move along in a constant stoop catching up armfuls of the stalks and binding them together into bundles with a quick twist of one of the long leaves. My sister, Teresa, and I didn't complain, for if we had, we'd have suffered a tongue-lashing and maybe even a swat on the behind. In truth, there was no cause for us to complain. We were young, our backs strong and supple and used to the work. It's true our bones might ache at the end of the day, but by the next morning we would be in fine form again. We both knew, I suppose, that a day would come when we would be bent and crippled like the crones in our settlement who'd spent their youth as we were doing. At that time, though, we didn't think of such things so far in the future. That is not to say that we weren't happy for the excuse to halt our work when the gentleman approached on his fine gelding with his dark velvet cloak flying behind him like the sail of a great ship.

Teresa, who was only ten, saw him first. "There he is again," she whispered as she picked up several stalks of grain. "That man we saw. The one who looked at you so strangely. Remember? The one who gave you the—"

I glanced up at him, and immediately my heart lodged in my throat. "Shush!" I said. "Papa will hear you." It wouldn't do for him to know that I had, indeed, seen the man before, and that I had even spoken to him.

2

It happened on a market day inside the walls of San Severino, the town nearest the fields we farm for the Duke of Angeni for a share of the harvest. We were all there at the market the day I saw him, Teresa and I and Papa and Mama with little Bernardino, who was still a suckling babe. Bernardino was weak and sickly, and the constant care he required had made Mama an invalid. At least, that was what Papa said, but when I saw the dullness of her eyes and the gray of her skin, and when I saw that she couldn't keep down most of the food she ate, I was afraid that there was something else that sickened her. I didn't speak of this aloud, though, because I didn't want to frighten Teresa. She was still a child, and she was gentle and timid. I always felt the need to protect her. Even when she annoyed me.

Teresa was small of bone and as fragile as Mama. Her eyes were the color of acorns and her hair a dark, curly mass. Except for the color of our hair, a person might not know we were sisters, since I was tall for my age, my hair straight, and my eyes more the green of an oak leaf than the brown of an acorn. I was not at all fragile like Teresa and Mama.

Mama's sickness, along with Bernardino's need for her, was what kept her out of the fields. It was also rare for her to make the long walk to the town for market, but on that particular day she was there, and she had agreed to mind the stand we'd secured to sell our few vegetables and cheese and eggs to the merchants' wives and others who came to the market.

3

"Run along, the two of you, and have a look at the wares." Mama waved us off with one of her frail and roughened hands. "But mind you're back here before the sun is halfway down the west."

Teresa and I could hardly contain our excitement. It was rare that we ever had the chance to wander through the market lanes, since it was usually our duty to mind the stand. We passed bakers selling their dark, coarse bread, and we caught the fresh, wet scent of the blood of calves and lambs and wild game being butchered. We saw great heaps of butter oozing dewdrops of milk, tall mounds of cheese growing sticky in the heat. There were baskets of turnips and leeks and beets, and piles of woolen and flaxen cloth woven by peasants like my mother. There was the sweet, fresh smell of bundles of hay and straw. We hurried past all of it, eager to see the new wares from far away that only the wealthy could afford to buy—the likes of merchants and bankers and notaries and such. We'd heard there were spices with the scent and taste of faraway lands as well as strange vegetables and fruits made of sweet water the color of gold.

We found one of the spices almost immediately. "Look!" Teresa whispered, tugging at my arm. "Those small rounds of bark. That's where the scent is coming from."

I could smell it, too. The scent lodged deep in my nostrils, near my throat. I had tasted pepper once, and the scent of this spice reminded me of that prickly sensation, yet it was faintly sweet at the same time.

4

"Shave off a bit and add it to sweetmeats or pies," the vendor said as he handed some of the bark to a woman. I could tell by her dress she was not a peasant as we were, but most likely a merchant's wife. " 'Twill give it a taste that would seduce a monk." The vendor gave her a wink.

"Ah, but will it work as well on my husband?" the woman asked with a little wink of her own. She was a handsome woman, well fed and rosy of face.

The vendor laughed and handed her another piece of the bark without charging her another *grano*. As he did so, he leaned toward her and whispered something in her ear that made them both laugh.

The thought passed my mind that now would be the time to snitch a bit of the bark, since the vendor was distracted. I didn't plan to steal a great quantity, mind you, just enough to provide a taste for Teresa and me.

My hand was raised and ready, but I stopped before I even got close to the prize when I saw someone looking at me. It was the gentleman I mentioned earlier. He was wearing a blue brocade cloak and a set of gold brocade sleeves. His clothing was so fine and beautiful I didn't notice his face at first, but when I did look at him I saw that he had a fine head of dark hair beneath a black cap. Though I could see a bit of gray in his hair, I sensed that he was not as old as Papa. His face was perhaps a bit too thin and his mouth too pinched, yet his countenance was not altogether unpleasant, and I think he would be called handsome.

I was awed by the golden water that dribbled down his chin. I knew immediately when I saw the round, slightly shriveled ball that was the color of marigolds, that he was eating one of the strange fruits Teresa and I had heard of.

"Would you like an orange?" he asked, pulling another of the fruits from his sleeve and handing it to me. He spoke in Italian, and the word he used was *arancia*. I had never heard the word before, but I couldn't stop myself from repeating it.

"*Arancia*," I said. The feel of the word dancing with my tongue made it seem as if I could taste its golden water. "It is beautiful."

"Yes, beautiful indeed," he said. "As beautiful as you. Have a taste."

I hesitated a moment, knowing I should turn away, but the temptation to taste the lovely fruit was too great for me. I reached for it and brought it to my lips, thinking I would have just one bite, then offer some to Teresa.

The smell was pungent and exciting, but the bitter taste surprised me and stiffened my jaw, and the sound of the man's laughter embarrassed me.

"No, no!" he cried. "You must remove the skin." I could see that he was peeling back the marigold covering of the fruit he held, but I didn't try the same with the fruit in my hand.

I dropped the beautiful orange, grabbed Teresa's hand, and ran away, back to our vending stall as quickly as I could. It wasn't easy to run, since Teresa kept pulling at my hand and arm as she turned around to look at the man.

"He's watching you. He's still watching you. And laughing."

"Don't look at him!" I gave her a quick jerk, forcing her to run with me.

Later, when we were back at our stall, Teresa kept pestering me with her whispered questions when she thought no one was paying attention to us.

"Did you hear him call you beautiful? Why did you run away?"

"Hush, Teresa."

"If you'd stayed I could have tasted that thing. I'll never have the chance again, and it's all your fault."

"It doesn't matter. Don't talk about it. Never speak of it again."

"You were embarrassed, weren't you? That's why you ran."

"I said don't speak of it!" I spoke to her as harshly as I could without attracting attention. It was true that I'd been embarrassed to act like the ignorant peasant that I was in front of the gentleman, but I also knew that if Teresa kept talking, our parents would ask questions, and I'd be ripe for a whipping for talking to a stranger who was above my station and for attempting to steal the spice. But Teresa wouldn't stop.

"What was the taste like when you brought it to your lips? Why was he laughing? Why was he looking at you like that?"

"What are the two of you whispering about?" Papa asked;

7

then, fortunately, before we had time to answer, he snarled at us again. "You've had your time to dally; now get to work. Both of you. Clean those eggs, and mind you don't break one."

I was nervous for the rest of the day, worried that Mama and Papa would somehow learn about the stranger and that I'd actually spoken to him, and especially that he'd seen me about to steal the exotic spice that looked like tree bark. After a while I saw that they were both too preoccupied with selling our eggs and cheese, and with the fact that, because eggs and cheese were so plentiful, we'd made only a few *granos* that day—not enough to buy hay for the animals or food for our own table. We rarely ate our own eggs or cheese, since it was far more profitable for us to sell them.

By the next morning I stopped worrying, and within a few days I'd completely forgotten about the stranger. On the day that he came riding into the field where Teresa and I were working with our father, I certainly wasn't thinking about him. My mind was filled with the events of the early morning.

I was the first one up that day, because it was my duty to feed the swine. Teresa had the easier job of feeding the chickens. She didn't have to fight off gaping, slobbering mouths and muck-encrusted bodies trying to knock the bucket of slops from her hands. Tending the swine was not my favorite thing to do, but I always got to it early, so I'd have it done in time to join Papa in the fields or to help Mama with the spinning, or whatever job fell to me. Papa would complain and threaten me with a whipping if I lolled about. Our landlord, the Duke of Angeni, allowed us the swine for ourselves, and I knew I should have been pleased that Papa trusted me to care for these important animals. After all, they provided what little meat we had, although it usually lasted only through the winter. We used practically every part of the animals, from the meat to the bladder to store the lard, to the hair, which my sister and I scraped off the carcasses at killing time each November, to be used as brushes or to mix with the plaster.

It's hard to think about how important the swine are when their stench fills your nostrils and they splatter your apron with their filth. That unpleasantness was all I could think of that morning—that and the fact that the late summer mornings were already bringing a chill to my bare arms and feet that made me wish for my bed of straw, warmed by Teresa's body and my heavy woolen coverlet.

The sound of a voice calling my name startled me out of my misery.

"Margherita! I knew I'd find you here." I recognized the voice. It belonged to Augustino, and the sound of it wouldn't have startled me at all had it not been such a soft sound, like the muted call of a wolf deep in the woods. At the same time, he grabbed my forearms from behind.

"Augustino! What are you doing here?" I tried to sound angry, but in truth I enjoyed the warmth of his work-hardened palms on my bare skin.

He spun me around until I was facing him. "Waiting for you, my pretty little swineherd." He tried to pull me closer, but I pushed him back.

"Can't you think of a prettier name for me?" I said.

"Oh, all right. How about lips-of-honey or breasts-like-pillows?" His hand cupped my left breast as he spoke, and he massaged it, teasing the nipple with the tip of his fingers. I liked the feel of it and leaned toward him, letting him kiss me full on the mouth.

As his mouth and his hands became more and more impassioned, I felt something warm and sweet coursing through my body, and I had to cling to him to keep from falling. Finally I was able to summon my strength and push away from him.

"Augustino, no. We mustn't . . ."

"Mustn't what, my little Rita? Mustn't act as if we care for each other? Mustn't do what is natural for a man and a maid?" He nuzzled my neck as he spoke, making little bites with his teeth that made me shiver.

"You know what I mean. We mustn't go any further than . . . I don't want to disgrace my family, and if you should get a child on me, 'twould not be suitable, since I'm not pledged to you or . . ." I was finding it difficult to concentrate, and instead of backing away from him, as I knew I should, I was melting into his arms.

"There would be no disgrace, my little swineherd. I would marry you. I will marry you today if you wish."

His words caught me completely off guard, and I couldn't think of what to say. We had kissed and explored each other's bodies before, but I had never let it go further than that, and never had he mentioned marriage to me.

"Augustino! Do you mean what you say?" I had visions of my own cottage, my own garden, my own children. We would be as poor as any other peasant who worked the land for the duke, but with Augustino I knew I would be as happy as if I were a noble lady in a grand palace. And what would it matter if he made me pregnant? There would be no disgrace if I were pledged to him. Most of the young women I knew were pregnant on their wedding day.

"Hush now," he whispered. "There'll be time for talk later." As he said that, he lifted my skirt with a quick flip of his hand and touched me in a place I had never allowed him to touch me before. A little cry of delight escaped my throat and then another as he thrust his fingers inside me. "Come with me," he said, leading me toward a stack of straw, both of us stumbling as we moved because we couldn't stop kissing each other.

I can't remember how it happened that I had no clothes on and that Augustino was wearing only his tunic. I do remember, though, how his mouth moved over my body, sucking, biting, kissing. I remember how he coaxed me to feel his naked hardness that, in the past, I had felt only with the back of my hand through his clothes. And then there was the delicious pain of the moment he entered me, and there was the way he moved

11

and the way I learned in that moment to move with him, and then, at last, the shudder that ran the length of both of us. He rolled off of me and lay beside me, breathing hard. I nestled my head on his chest and wished that he would say something to me. We lay that way for what seemed only a moment before he turned toward me and kissed me, and before I knew it we were doing the same thing again, only slower. This time the heat simmered for a long, delicious time before it burst into flame.

A ribbon of soft sunlight showed itself on the horizon and brought me to my senses. I scrambled to my feet and scooped up my dress and apron.

"The sun's up. Papa will already be in the field with the sickle!" I hurried toward the door, but Augustino grabbed my hand. He spoke two words.

"Tomorrow morning?"

I hesitated a moment, then smiled at him. "Tomorrow morning," I whispered.

I dressed quickly; then, grabbing my slop pail, I ran toward the house, and I felt a brief moment of relief when I saw Papa's sickle leaning against the exterior stone wall. That meant he hadn't yet gone to the field. My relief was short-lived, and my heart was pounding with fear as I stepped inside the house with my pail. Perhaps he hadn't left because he was waiting for me, waiting to question me about why I had taken so long with the swine.

He was sitting at the table just finishing his breakfast pottage, and Teresa was sitting on the floor near the fireplace holding a ball of string above little Bernardino's cradle, teasing him as he tried to reach for it. I was thankful, everything seemed to be moving at a slow pace that morning. Papa had hardly noticed that I'd come inside the house, and there was no indication that he observed or cared that I was later than usual. Only Mama, I thought, looked at me a little strangely as she glanced up from the pot she was stirring over the fire. But she couldn't possibly know what I'd been doing, could she? Couldn't possibly know about the sticky feel between my legs where the blood of my maidenhead mingled with Augustino's seed.

Papa stood up from the table and reached for his tunic. "Time to get to the fields, girls. Teresa, leave the babe alone. There'll be time to tease him this winter when the days are dark and there's no fieldwork to do. Margherita, I trust you've had your pottage."

"Yes, Papa," I lied. I had not, in fact, taken the time to eat before I went to tend the swine, but if I admitted that, questions might be raised about what I'd been doing all morning. Perhaps it was just as well that I didn't eat anyway. I knew that our market day had been less than what Mama and Papa had hoped. There would be little money for food, and most of what we raised would need to be sold. Many's the day we'd all gone hungry before, but even at that, we were luckier than some whose children died of the bone sickness and whose women

13

fainted in the field, all from lack of nourishment. I didn't mind, really. A day of hunger now and then was nothing to worry about.

As I worked in the fields that morning, I hardly noticed my empty stomach. My head was too filled with the delicious memory of the few moments I'd spent with Augustino as well as with the undeniable fact that I knew I was a woman now and that soon I would be a wife.

And then, when I saw the stranger on his fine horse riding up to us that day, my happy mood changed abruptly. As I mentioned, I was suddenly reminded of my attempt to steal the exotic bark a few days earlier, and I feared he'd come to confront me with that, and most likely my father as well. My chest felt tight, and I was unable to draw a proper breath.

Perhaps God was punishing me for my sins. Like Eve, who had been seduced by her own forbidden fruit.

"Look!" Teresa whispered. "He's looking at you!"

Indeed he was, and smiling as well. I shifted my eyes away from him and kept my head down as I went back to picking up the stalks of grain Papa cut with his sickle. I felt bile rush to my throat as soon as he spoke.

"You there!" He pointed one of his fine-gloved hands at my father. "A word with you!"

Papa glanced up from his work with a surprised expression, but, mindful of his station, dropped his sickle and approached the stranger. The man remained on his horse, looking down at Papa as he spoke. Try as I might, I couldn't make out any of the words they said to each other. Finally Papa turned to us.

"To the cottage. Both of you. See what you might do to help your mother. Tell her I'll be along soon enough."

Teresa pestered me all during the short walk to the cottage. "What does the man want, Margherita?"

"How should I know?" My words came out sounding cross.

"He saw you try to steal that funny spice."

"That's ridiculous," I said, sounding even angrier. "He couldn't possibly have seen me." Perhaps I thought if I denied it aloud it wouldn't be true.

"Yes, he did. I saw him looking. Do you think he's telling Papa?"

"Shush, Teresa."

With that she began to cry. "I don't want you to be sent to prison, Rita. You would die there, and all because of a bit of nasty old spice you didn't even manage to take."

"I told you to shush, Teresa. I'm not going to be sent to prison."

"Are you sure?"

"Of course I'm sure." I had lied again. I had no idea what my punishment would be, or if it would stand in my favor that I hadn't actually gotten my hands on the strange stuff.

When we got back to the house, Mama was quite curious about the stranger and kept asking us questions we couldn't an-

15

swer, such as where he'd come from; did he say what he wanted; and did Papa look worried or frightened? I was both surprised and thankful that Teresa at least had the wisdom to keep what little she did know to herself. What good would it have done to have told Mama anyway? In her frail condition any additional worry would probably have only sickened her more.

Later that night when Papa finally came home, he said not a word about the stranger to either Teresa or me, but when we were all in bed I could hear him talking to Mama in low, murmured tones and hear her respond in the same quiet way. Although we had but one room and our beds were close together, they spoke so softly it was impossible to hear them.

The next morning when I went to my chores with the swine, Augustino was there again, and we went once again to our bed of straw, where he made me forget, at least for a little while, about the stranger and what business he might have had with Papa. When I got back to the house, Mama once again looked at me with that expression that made me feel as if she could see my thoughts, but along with that, this time there was an odd sadness in her eyes.

Papa didn't mention the stranger at all as we worked that day, nor did he mention him when we quit for our supper and rest. By the next morning I had all but forgotten about him, and I got up extra early to meet Augustino. All day long as I worked in the fields, my mind spun the tale of the morning's events with him over and over again in minute detail until I felt myself wanting him in a way I had never experienced. I spent the rest of the day trying to contrive a way to meet him during the night.

It was later that evening at supper that Papa told me about the contract he had made with the stranger, whose name, he said, was Dominico Vasari.

"You will be his wife," he said. "It is a good contract. He requires no dowry, and he has paid me well."

I couldn't breathe, and I felt my body grow cold as death. Peasants did not make contracts to marry the way the rich and powerful did. Girls like me were free to choose their own mates.

Mama, who had kept her head down until now, looked up at me and tried to smile. Finally she reached with one of her hands to touch mine.

"You will be the wife of a gentleman," she whispered.

Chapter 2

My MOTHER was smiling, but I could see tears glistening in her eyes. "You will have gowns of silk and satin. Your children will never be hungry." She squeezed my hand, then touched my face.

I shrank back from her, hurt and angry that she thought so little of me that she would pretend to be happy when my father had just sold me to a stranger. Mama dropped her hand and started to speak, but instead bit her lip.

"You're fortunate, *ragazza*," my father said. "And you've made us fortunate!" He didn't have to pretend to be happy. His smile made a wide gash of his mouth, and I sensed he could hardly keep a laugh from popping. "I didn't have to do a thing. He came to *me*. Imagine that! And he asks for no dowry." He chuckled. "Said you were all he needed. Said he saw you at market and knew at once. . . ." He gave me a mandatory frown. "You weren't doing anything improper for the gentleman, were you?" Before I could answer, he continued with his delighted chatter. "A pretty penny he gave us. We'll not be hurting for a while. But mind you don't disappoint the gentleman. You be a good wife, *ragazza*. And what cause would you have not to be? You'll be wanting for nothing."

19

"When . . . when must I leave?" I finally managed to ask, but I thought I would choke on the words.

"He'll send for you," my father said. "That's the way gentlemen do things. They *send* for you. There'll be a wedding, of course. I was firm on that. 'You'll not take my daughter away to live in sin,' I says to him. 'There'll be a priest,' I says." My father's sudden piousness made me feel ill, since he always slept through Mass. "Oh, it'll be a grand wedding, I'm sure," he continued. "Just you wait. Even the duke will be impressed. Of course, he'll be invited."

"And the rest of us?" Mama's voice was timid, almost frightened, and a stark contrast to Papa's boisterousness.

"The rest of us? What do you mean, woman?" He was fairly bellowing now, and he pounded my mother's back. "You'll be in the front and in a fine gown, I daresay. You'll be the envy of all of them."

Mama's expression didn't change. She'd never owned a fine gown. No one we knew had a fine gown. Some of the more fortunate among us had an extra dress of coarse wool to wear when the other had to be washed, but no fine gown. I watched my mother, wondering what sort of dress she was imagining. It was impossible to tell. Her only response was to pull Teresa close to her and to drop her eyes, unable to look at me. Teresa began to cry.

"Hush, my little one," Mama said in a soothing voice. "You shall have a fine gown for the grand wedding yourself."

Was that all they could think of? Their fine gowns and a place at the front of the church? What of me? I wanted to scream that question at them. What of me, being sold to a stranger? What did I know of how to live in the house of a gentleman? What would become of me?

I didn't speak a word of what I felt, though. I was far too frightened to speak. I could only look at all of them with the anger and fear I felt, and yes, hatred, too, because my own family had betrayed me. I thought of running away. I could go to Augustino. He had said he would marry me. But how could we do that now? My father would never consent to it, and even if I did manage somehow to wed Augustino, Papa would only drag me back home and punish me for going against his wishes. Perhaps we could escape to another village. But how would we manage to live? Augustino was obligated to the Duke of Angeni. No other landlord would be likely to take us. But there had to be a way. If only I could find Augustino, he would think of something.

I made a plan to wait until the others were asleep, and then I would slip away and go to the cottage where Augustino lived with his family. I would awaken him, although I wasn't sure how I would do it without waking his family. I would find a way, though, and I would tell him what had happened. He would know what to do. That half-formed plan was the only thing that kept me from sinking into despair as I waited for everyone to sleep.

It seemed to take forever before I heard the soft, rhythmic breathing that meant Teresa and Mama were asleep, the gentle sucking noise from Bernardino with his thumb in his mouth, and the snores from my father. I raised myself from my pallet where I lay next to Teresa and tiptoed in my bare feet across the hard-packed earth that was our floor, trying not to disturb anyone. Our cottage was small, and I knew it well enough to avoid, even in darkness, bumping into a bench or table or cooking pot. At last I reached the door and swung it out slowly and carefully on its rope hinges, then stepped out into the black, starlit night.

I sucked in my breath, ready to scream, when I saw the form that suddenly materialized in front of me in the dim light. I stood still, as if I were frozen, too frightened to move or speak. I wasn't certain whether the form was human or demon until I heard the soft voice of my mother.

"Don't go, Margherita. Not tonight."

"But I was only going to relieve myself behind the—"

"You can tell him good-bye in the morning."

"Tell who good-bye? I just need to . . ." I stopped speaking, too confused to continue. She couldn't possibly know about Augustino.

"I know this is hard for you. I remember how frightened I was when I married your father."

"But you weren't sent away. You stayed here. I don't want to go away. I want to stay here and . . . and marry someone else."

"You will be better off in the city with Dominico Vasari than you would be with Augustino."

"Augustino? How . . . how did you know . . . ?"

"Hush, child." She pulled me toward her and took me in her arms. "I've seen the way he looks at you. Seen the flush on your face these recent mornings when you come in after being so long at your chores. A mother knows, Margherita. You will see. A mother knows. Especially when it's her firstborn daughter."

I pushed her away. "You're wrong! I *won't* be better off with . . . whatever his name is. I love Augustino, and he loves me, and he has told me he will marry me."

"Margherita, keep your voice down. You don't want to wake your father." Her own voice was soft, almost a whisper. "And listen to me, please. Augustino is a boy and only a poor peasant. Think of how your life will be with him. How it has always been with us. Think of how it could be if—"

"You don't understand, Mama. You don't know what it's like to love someone. To want to be with him all of the time. You don't know how it is with Augustino and me."

My mother didn't respond, and her silence made me afraid for a reason I couldn't understand. Finally she spoke. "I was young once, too," she said, and turned away from me, moving toward the door.

I stood alone in the darkness, wondering what she meant by that. Did she think my feelings for Augustino were nothing more than the foolish yearnings of the young? If she did, she was wrong. I was certain of that. No one on earth had ever felt about another person the way I felt about Augustino.

I turned and ran away from our little house, stumbling in the darkness until I found the lane that led to the equally small house where Augustino lived with his family—his father, Jacobo, and his mother, Dolcina, and his five brothers and sisters. Since it was late summer, the one window in the cottage was still open and not latched shut, as it would have been in cold weather. I walked to the window and peered inside. At first all I could see were dark lumps where the family lay on pallets on the floor. The fire had been banked and smoldered just as it did in any peasant's cottage, even in summer, waiting to be rekindled for the morning. The few glowing embers provided the only light in the small room. It was not just luck, I thought at the time, but divine providence that Augustino should be the one lying closest to the glowing embers so that I was able to distinguish his features.

I stooped down and picked up a soft clod of dirt and tossed it through the window so it landed directly on his head. He stirred slightly, then turned on his side, his face toward the fireplace, still asleep. I picked up another clod and threw it. This time it landed on his cheek. He stirred again, swiping at his cheek with his hand.

I signaled him. "Pssst!"

He sat up, looked around, and when I signaled again he saw me. He stood, and, wrapping the blanket he'd been lying

on around his shoulders, he stepped over the other sleeping
bodies on the floor and slipped out of the door to meet me.

"Margherita! What are you doing here?"

"I have to talk to you." We were both whispering.

He took my arm and led me away from the window. "What
is it?" he asked when we were a good distance away.

Emotions overwhelmed me, and all I could do was throw
my arms around him. He seemed surprised, but he responded
by pulling me close to him. He caressed me and moved his
hands down my back to my buttocks, then up again to my
waist and breasts, and I realized he thought I'd come to him for
another reason.

I pushed him away. "No! We have to talk."

"Talk?" He said the word as if he'd never heard of it before.

"Yes, something dreadful has happened."

"We can talk about it later," he said, and tried to embrace
me again. He seemed capable of only one thought.

"Augustino! Listen to me." I was busy fighting his hands.

"What?" He sounded petulant.

"My father has given me to another man." I started to cry
and could hardly manage to speak the next words. "The . . . the
contract—it's already been signed. I'm to be married soon."

"Shhh!" He clamped his hand over my mouth as my sobs
grew louder. "You'll wake everyone."

I sniffed. "Did you hear what I said?" I was beginning to
think he was slow-witted.

"You're to be married?" he asked. "Who? Who will you marry?"

"I don't know. Some gentleman from town. His name is Vasari, I think." The air had turned a little cooler, and I was shivering, wishing Augustino would offer to share his blanket with me.

"A gentleman, you say? Then I'll bet he paid a pretty penny, didn't he? Your father must be a happy man!"

"Augustino!"

"I didn't mean . . . I meant nothin' by it," he said, reminding me of a little boy. There was a pause before he added, "Does this mean we can't do it anymore?"

"Oooh!" I said, repelled. I turned away from him, prepared to find my way back home.

"Wait!" He grasped my shoulder to halt me and turned me around. "Don't be mad, Rita. I just meant, well, you know, I was just wondering if—"

I tried to wrench myself free of his grasp. "Is that all you ever think of?"

"What?" He sounded genuinely puzzled. "Oh, well, no, of course not. Sometimes I think about kissing you, and sometimes about how your nipple feels in my mouth, or—"

"You're disgusting!"

"Why is that disgusting?" Once again he sounded puzzled. "I thought you liked it, too. I thought you loved me."

"And I thought you loved me. I thought you wanted to marry me."

26

"How can I marry you if your father has signed a contract to give you to someone else?"

"You're thick-witted, Augustino. I'm better off *not* marrying you." I made no attempt to keep my voice down, and at the moment I didn't care who heard me. I jerked away, making certain I freed myself of him this time, and ran toward home.

Augustino caught up with me in two long strides, stopping me and once again turning me around to face him. "Rita! My beautiful Rita with breasts like pillows and a mouth like honey . . ."

"Your sweet words won't work this time. You only say them so I'll lie with you."

"I say them because I love you."

I tried to see his face to try to tell whether or not he was telling the truth, but the night was too dark. "Oh, Augustino . . ."

"And of course I would marry you if I could."

"My father would never permit—"

"No, he wouldn't."

"But we could run away."

"Yes," he said. "We could do that." He didn't sound very enthusiastic. After a pause, he added, "Where will we go?"

I didn't know how to answer that. I had foolishly hoped he would know, and all I could do now was burst into tears yet another time. At least he had the decency to put his arms around me and croon things to me that he thought would comfort me—things such as, "We'll think of something. Maybe tomorrow. Don't cry. Don't worry."

Finally I stopped crying, and when I whispered to him, "I don't want to go home," without a word he led me away. I had no idea where we were going, and I was surprised when I realized he was leading me up the steps to the chapel where we go for Mass and the priest's irregular visits.

"Augustino, what—"

"Shhh," he said.

The building was cool, almost cold, no warmer than the air outside, but we huddled together on the hard stone floor under his blanket in a corner near the back. I wondered how he had thought of coming to the chapel. Had he been here before at night with someone else? I pushed that question from my mind and let him hold me next to him as we sat on the stone floor and leaned against the wall. He fell asleep quickly while I was still wide-awake, but I put my head on his shoulder and tried not to think of anything except the sound of his breathing and how warm and comforting his arms felt encircling me.

Just before dawn I woke him. "We have to go," I said. "Before someone finds us here."

He looked at me with bleary eyes and a confused, questioning look, as if he couldn't remember where he was or even who I might be. "Oh!" he said finally. "Yes, before someone finds us." He scrambled to his feet and, as an afterthought, helped me up.

Together we hurried out of the chapel. We came to his family's cottage first, but he stopped before we reached the door.

"You'd best not come any closer." He was breathing hard after our sprint. "Go home, and I'll come to you later."

"Yes," I said, my own breath coming in short gasps. "Yes, later."

He gave me a quick kiss on my forehead and hurried away toward his family's cottage. I watched him until he was out of sight, still full of hope that he would somehow save me like the bold and gallant knights in the stories I sometimes heard peddlers telling in the marketplace.

Back home I went straight to my chores and finished quickly. This time when I entered the house my mother only glanced at me briefly and went back to tending to Bernardino. I ate the coarse bread and pottage she had put out for our breakfast and drank a cup of goat's milk. The whole time I hardly looked at my father, who, oddly enough, lingered in his bed awhile before he rose and pulled off some of the bread for himself, then busied himself honing the blade of his sickle to a fine edge. He spoke only once to me the whole time.

"Fed the swine, have you, Margherita?"

"Yes," I said, not minding that my answer came out short and petulant.

I went back to ignoring him and occupied myself with tying my hair back with a scarf and helping Teresa tie hers in the way we always did before going for our day of work in the fields. I was still trying to get Teresa's unruly curls under the scarf when my father spoke again.

"Put your scarves away, girls. You won't be needing them today."

I looked at him, surprised.

"It won't do for him to find you sweating in the fields," he added.

"He's coming today?" My voice sounded choked. I'd expected more time. Would Augustino arrive in time to rescue me?

He didn't answer me directly. "Take off that dirty apron and rub the spots off your dress. Comb your hair and wash your face, too. You must look your best so he won't be tempted to change his mind."

For the first time that morning, my mother's eyes met mine. I wasn't certain what I saw there. Was it anger? Regret? Pity? Or a warning? Did she know I expected Augustino to come? It didn't matter. I was too occupied with my own emotions of anger and fear to care what she thought. I took off my apron and threw it toward a bench, not caring where it landed, but I made no attempt to comb my hair or wash my face. As for the spots on my dress, I only looked at them, wishing there were more and that they were even darker so Dominico Vasari would be disgusted by them.

Mama walked over to where I had slumped on the floor and was leaning against the fireplace. She made an attempt to smooth my hair with her hand, but as soon as she touched my hair I stood up and, without speaking to her, walked out the door. Teresa followed me, but I pretended not to see her and sat down on a large tree stump next to a rain barrel.

In a little while she nestled against me and spoke to me in a timid voice. "Where will you go? Will it be far away?"

"How should I know?" Anger made my words sound clipped. I kept my eyes on the lane, hoping to see Augustino approaching.

Teresa suddenly put her arms around me and buried her face in my shoulder. Hard sobs made her body shake. It was enough to soften my heart and bring me out of my self-pity.

"It's all right, little sister," I said, stroking her hair. "Perhaps something will happen and I won't have to go."

Teresa sniffed and raised her head to look at me. "Something like a miracle? Like when the Blessed Mother appears and talks to people?"

"I don't know. Maybe."

"The Blessed Mother is coming?"

"Someone else, maybe." I was still watching the lane for Augustino, but there was no one in sight.

"But what if the Blessed Mother doesn't come? And what if no one else comes to help you? You'll go away and I'll never see you again."

"Of course you will. You can come visit me." I suddenly realized how much I would miss her. I had no intention of going away with the stranger, but if Augustino and I ran away, would

I never see Teresa and little Bernardino again? I couldn't bear to think that I wouldn't.

"I shall send for you." I was desperate to comfort her, and, without thinking, I said the first thing that came into my mind. "A servant leading a fine horse for you to ride will come for you and bring you to me."

"And Mama, too? Can the servant bring a fine horse for her, too?"

I hesitated a moment. I was still angry with Papa for signing the contract and with Mama for not protesting, but I had to think of Teresa. "Of course," I said. "Mama will come, too."

"I still don't want you to go," Teresa said and began to cry again.

I stroked her hair for a moment, but I didn't speak. I had seen someone approaching a long way down the lane. I didn't take my eyes off of the distant figure, and I was certain it was Augustino coming to rescue me. The longer I watched, the more certain I was that I was wrong. The person coming toward us was on a horse. Augustino had no horse. Neither did he have a fine velvet cloak to fly behind him like a sail in the wind.

Chapter 3

MASTER VASARI didn't see Teresa and me at first, since we were several yards away from the house. Perhaps he wouldn't have seen us at all if Teresa's voice hadn't been so loud with excitement when she called out, "Look! It's the stranger! He's come to marry you and take you away."

At times I've allowed myself to wonder what my life might have been like if he hadn't heard her voice and turned first his head to see us and then his fine horse to ride up in front of us. Perhaps I could have run away. And what would have happened to me then? Would I have found happiness? Might I have been killed by brigands or kidnapped for immoral purposes? I know now that it is useless to have such thoughts. It was the will of the Almighty that Master Vasari should have been sitting there atop his chestnut gelding, his handsome face looking down at me, and smiling at me with his hard mouth.

He was dressed in clothes that were even finer than the ones I'd seen him wear before. This time his sleeves and cloak were crimson brocade and his tunic made of brown wool that looked softer than duck's down.

"Good morning, Margherita. I see you're up early."

I looked down at my feet and refused to say anything. Teresa, who was even shyer than I, didn't speak either. He moved his great horse closer to me and reached down to grasp my chin and raise my face so that my eyes met his. "You shall sleep as late as you like, once you are my bride." He gave my chin a little tug and turned his horse away, riding the short distance to the front of our cottage.

"Has he come to take you away *now?*" Teresa's voice was a soft, frightened whisper.

"No! I'm not leaving today." There was fear in my own voice, but I couldn't see how it was possible for me to be an ordinary peasant one day and taken away by a strange gentleman and expected to be a lady the next day. Even if I should consent to leave, which I wasn't about to do, we still had to have the wedding. But there wasn't going to be a wedding, I told myself, except the simple one I would have when I married Augustino. Where was Augustino? I turned my face once again toward the lane that led to his house, but there was still no one in sight.

Teresa almost drove me mad with her questions as we sat there. "Why do you keep looking at the lane? Is someone else coming? Is the stranger talking to Papa? What are they talking about? Are they discussing your wedding? What of the gown I shall wear? Can I have a blue one? Are they deciding that? Oh, I wish I could listen!"

I left her questions unanswered and did my best to ignore her until Papa appeared at the door of the cottage and shouted my name, then motioned for me to come inside. It was precisely at that moment that I once again saw something approaching along the lane in the distance. It was an enormous thing lumbering along. Something I didn't recognize. It couldn't be Augustino.

Teresa saw it, too. "Look," she whispered, and tugged at my arm. "What is that thing? Has the devil come for us?"

It could have been the devil, for all I knew. It was close enough now that I could see that it was creating a cloud of dust as it approached. I wanted desperately to keep my eyes on it, at least for a little while, but Papa's shouts became louder and more demanding. I tore my eyes from the lane and ran into the cottage. Teresa followed closely, obviously too frightened by the strange sight to stay by herself.

Once we were inside the cottage, I wanted to tell someone about what Teresa and I had seen on the lane, but I felt too shy to speak in the presence of the stranger. It didn't matter, I suppose, since I couldn't have found the words to express what I wanted to say.

The stranger—I still thought of him that way, even though I knew by now, of course, that his name was Dominico Vasari—sat alone on a bench near the table with his back to the fire. His legs were crossed, showing off his fine hose. One arm rested on the table so that his pose suggested pictures I'd seen in one of the market booths of a monarch in repose, except that I noticed one of his fine sleeves had soaked up a spot of grease from the table. I tried not to meet his eyes with my own, but it was difficult not to, so overpowering was his gaze.

He spoke my name as a way of acknowledging me, all the while staring at me. I managed a little curtsy of the kind I'd been taught to make on the rare occasions I encountered our landlord, the Duke of Angeni. That made him smile, and I noticed that even his eyes were smiling, all of which should have made me relax, but I still found it impossible. His very presence made me tense.

"Cuts a fine figure, that girl," my father said. "And she's strong, too. Don't mind them skinny arms. They mean nothing. Why, I've seen her lift two pails of slops for the swine and think nothing of it. And her hips? Rounded like her mother's, as you can see. Made for birthing, she is. Sons, I have no doubt, and she's—"

"I don't want you to be so frightened, Margherita," the stranger said, interrupting my father. It was a rude thing to do, but I supposed then that gentlemen had a right to be rude. "There's no need for you to be frightened, because I shall make you happy. You'll see. And in time I'll teach you proper manners so there'll be nothing to remind anyone of the filth and roughness you come from."

It was my turn to stare at him now. I had no idea what to think of what he had just said to me. It appeared that a part of what he was saying was pure kindness, but that he had just insulted me as well. It seemed to me that a gentleman had no right to insult his bride. I might have been upset by that, except that it gave me a faint glimmer of hope. If he thought I was filthy and rough, then maybe he would change his mind about marrying me. It was going through my head what I might do to make him think I was impossibly filthy and rough when my father shouted at me.

"Straighten up, wench. Be on your best behavior. They's a gentleman before you."

So conditioned was I to doing my father's bidding that I immediately straightened my shoulders and sent a hand up to smooth my hair, although I swear it was against my own will. My actions made the gentleman chuckle.

"You'll do," he said, rising from the bench. "Not only are you a fine-looking specimen, but you train well, too." The way he studied me with his eyes made me feel as if I were a prized heifer on display in the marketplace.

A sudden racket made him lift his gaze from me and look out the window that was open above the door. We'd all heard the same thing and tried to see what was out there. It took a few seconds for it to come into full view of the window, and what we saw made every one of us, except Master Vasari, of course, suck in our breath in amazement. There in front of our cottage was a cart. The largest cart I'd ever seen. It was pulled by two bay horses, and there was a peaked covering of some heavy blue material over it just behind where the driver sat. I had never seen such a sight, but I realized this was what had been lumbering down the road and stirring up dust.

By now it had attracted the attention of some of the other peasants who lived nearby. People were coming out of their houses and walking in from the fields to stare at the elaborate cart. I stretched my neck to try to determine whether Augustino was among them, but I couldn't make him out.

"As you see, I've sent a cart to take Margherita to my house in town," Master Vasari said. He reached for my arm. "Come along, my dear. And thank you for your cooperation," he said, turning back to my father. He led me forcibly toward the door. I did my best to hold back, but he held my arm so tightly it was hurting, and I couldn't help but give in to his tugging.

"Forgive me, sir," my father said, taking a hesitant step toward us.

"Yes." Master Vasari sounded annoyed.

"Umm, sir, about the . . . well, the wedding, sir . . ."

"Of course, the wedding," Master Vasari said. "I gave you my word as a gentleman that I would treat your daughter honorably, and so I shall. Of course there'll be a wedding. A grand wedding. You need not worry about that."

"Yes. Yes, of course," my father said, all but groveling. "But we . . . that is, well, we would like to know . . . Pardon me, sir, but, as you know, we are her family and we expect to attend."

Master Vasari gave my father an odd look, as if he might be speaking some foreign tongue. "You expect . . ." He laughed.

"You expect to attend?" He shook his head. "My good fellow, surely you know how difficult that would be. Your daughter will soon become a lady. Those at her wedding will be gentlemen and their ladies. I'm sure you understand how uncomfortable it would be for you—for all of us—if you were to . . . I'm sure you understand."

"Oh . . . oh, yes, of course," Papa said in his most servile manner. "You're right. We . . . I understand."

Master Vasari pulled on my arm again, tightening his grip so that it hurt even more. I caught a glimpse of my mother and thought I saw tears in her eyes. I did my best to hold back, but Master Vasari pulled me with a jerk, almost lifting me off my feet. I had no choice but to follow him out the door. He dragged me to the covered cart and forced me inside in a manner so rough that I almost cried out, but my pride would not allow it. I endured the bruising grip he had on my arm and the pain on my shins when I bumped them against the edge of the cart.

He all but tossed me inside, and when I landed on the hard seat I leaned forward, looking through the gap in the cover, hoping against hope that I would see Augustino. I caught not a glimpse of him before Master Vasari, who was in the cart with me, closed the dark curtain, shutting out the world. By now someone—the driver, I assumed—had tied Vasari's horse to the back of the cart.

I slumped down in my seat, refusing to look at my captor,

who sat on a narrow bench across from me, although I was keenly aware that he was looking at me. He mistook my petulance for shyness, I think, because he leaned toward me and lifted my chin, just as he had done before.

"I told you, my dirty little wench, that you need not be afraid. You are mine now. Don't you realize how fortunate you are?"

I still didn't speak, and, to my chagrin, I couldn't keep the tears from filling my eyes and running down my face. Master Vasari must have found my tears amusing, because he laughed. It was a quiet little chuckle, but I thought it cruel, nevertheless.

"I shall allow your tears this time, because I know you are like a puppy leaving the litter, but mind you, I won't put up with them again. I can't stand a sniveling wench." He straightened his back and folded his arms in front of him in a self-satisfied way. "But I suspect you won't think of crying much after today. There'll be no reason for you to miss anything you've known before. Not when you see what I have to offer you."

Although I must admit I was curious about all the things he might have to offer, I didn't respond, because, in spite of my curiosity, I was still frightened and angry. Instead I turned my face away and did my best to peer around the curtain to the outside. In a little while Master Vasari's chin was rolling on his chest in rhythm with the swaying of the cart. I pushed the curtain back for a better view, since, besides being curious about what might be in store for me, I was also a bit awed by our journey. The first part of the drive was familiar to me, since it was the same road we always took when we went to the market in San Severino—the same steep hillsides and woodlands interrupted by olive groves and fields of grain already harvested. Red ribbons of wild poppies stretched along the hillsides and lay in bunches on some of the meadows. I had not yet learned to appreciate the tranquillity of that kind of beauty.

It always took us more than half of the day to walk to the marketplace, and often longer, depending on the burdens we carried. Today, however, it couldn't have been more than three hours before the walls of the town were in sight, and in the next few minutes we were at the gate. It had been a rough and bumpy ride, and I would have much preferred walking, even if it took longer.

I had seen beggars outside the walls near the gate before. All of us, even Papa, always tried to give them a crust of bread if we had it to spare. I had never seen them as they were now, though. They rushed toward the cart, shouting and crying with their hands held out. The driver shouted back at them, and once I saw his whip lash out at a girl who got too close. The child couldn't have been any older than Teresa, and I clasped my hand over my mouth to keep from crying out. I leaned forward and tried to look around the curtain to see what had happened to her.

"What are you doing? Get your head back inside the cart!" It was Master Vasari's voice, and it startled me. I dropped the edge of the curtain and turned to face him. Apparently the commotion had awakened him.

"It's only the usual vermin." He stretched himself leisurely as he spoke. "You'll get used to them. Or perhaps you're already used to vermin." He laughed as he said that. If he'd made a joke I didn't understand it, and I still refused to speak.

In a little while we were rolling past the area I recognized as the market square, which wasn't a square at all, but was rather egg-shaped. It looked quite forlorn today with all the booths closed, and the crowds missing except for a few ragged souls milling around and stooping over now and then as if to pick something up.

I kept my eyes turned to the outside, and I was provided with more amazing sights. I saw what I thought must be dwellings unlike any cottage I'd ever seen where I lived. They were tall stone structures with rooms stacked on top of rooms in much the same way as in the Duke of Angeni's large house, except that these were more modest in size. The roofs were of a hard material, slate, I thought. The houses crowded out most of the trees, except for a few scattered here and there between the rows of buildings. In the distance I saw a church steeple. People walked along the streets, and some moved along in carts. Some looked to be as poor as I was. Others looked to be gentlemen and, occasionally, a lady.

In a little while the houses we passed were larger and surrounded by their own walls with towers, much like the duke's home. It was as if the inhabitants of each house had to protect themselves from their neighbors. At least there were gardens and orchards around the widely spaced houses, unlike the others we had passed.

When the driver stopped the cart to open a large gate, I was curious. Then when he drove the cart through the gate and stopped in front of one of the houses, I thought something had gone wrong until I saw Master Vasari stand and step out of the cart.

"Welcome to your new home," he said, and gave me his hand to help me out of the cart.

At first I thought I wouldn't accept his help, but he gave me no choice. He took my hand first, then quickly slipped both his hands under my arms and lifted me out of the cart as if I were a child. He sat me down on my feet in front of him and held me at arm's length. He shook his head, staring at me with an odd expression, as if he'd just smelled spoiled meat.

Still holding me apart from him, he shouted a name over his shoulder.

"Grimani! Grimani! Come here immediately."

Almost instantly a man of about my father's age came running to him. I couldn't tell from whence he'd come. He made a little bow and was about to speak when Master Vasari spoke instead.

"Take her to Lorenzia. Quick!"

The man, Grimani, bowed again, mumbled something, and took my arm. I stood my ground, refusing to move. Grimani gave his master a puzzled look and tugged at my arm again. Still I refused to move.

"She's stubborn," Master Vasari said, and at the same time gave me a whack across my buttocks that stung like a thousand bees and so startled me that I jumped forward just as a horse might have done. It gave Grimani the momentum he needed to pull me along, and I could hear Master Vasari laughing behind me.

Grimani pulled me inside the house and up a series of stone steps that were similar to the steps in front of the chapel where we attended Mass, except that they were steeper and narrower. They reminded me of the terraced fields along the mountainsides. We stopped in a great open space with ceilings that were higher than any I'd ever seen outside of a church. The walls were painted with scenes of ladies and gentlemen in grand gardens. It took me a moment to realize that some of the pictures represented stories from the Bible. I couldn't keep my eyes off of them and felt as if God himself might materialize from the walls and speak to me.

It was a woman who materialized in front of me. She was dressed in a fine woolen dress the color of smoke that fit her tightly at the waist and fell in ripples over her hips to the floor. It was rounded at the neck and sewn with a thin strip of brocade. The sleeves hugged her arms, and more strips of brocade were sewn to the wrists. She wore a soft white cap on her head.

"Is this it?" she asked.

Grimani nodded and mumbled, "Yes, signora."

"It will have to be washed," she said, looking me over while she waved Grimani away.

I watched him leave and then turned back to the signora, not knowing what I should do. She was still looking at me as one might look at a goat she was thinking of buying.

"Follow me," she said, and turned aside.

I followed her, for no other reason than that I didn't want to be left alone. She led me into a room hung with tapestries. There was a bed in the room such as I had never before seen. It was enormous and had some sort of soft purple covering on it.

"Take off your clothes," she said. At first I thought I had misunderstood her, but she said it again. "I said, take off your clothes. You're going to have a bath."

"A . . . a bath?" It was the first time I'd spoken since I left my home, and I might not have spoken that time except that I was shocked. I'd heard of the bathhouses in town. They were said to be places of sin. I had been told men visited the women's bathhouses for indiscriminate coupling, which was far different from what Augustino and I had done, since our coupling was done for love, not just lust, and besides, we were to be married.

"Yes," the signora said in her sharp, cutting tone. "You've never had a bath?" She pulled out a large wooden vat. I had no idea the purpose of it. "Well?" she demanded. "*Have* you?"

I finally managed to answer her. "Twice that I remember."

Chapter 4

NEVER BEFORE had I endured such humiliation. I stood naked before the signora while she busied herself with placing cloths of various sizes on a small table next to the wooden vat. She went to a chest and pulled out a hunk of tallow soap. I was quite familiar with that, at least, since I'd often helped my mother make it by boiling ashes with the fat of the swine after they were butchered. We sold it at market. Perhaps my mother and I had made the very piece I was looking at. That thought made me feel lonely and made me miss my family. I might have succumbed to tears if I hadn't been so frightened and awed by all that was happening to me.

The signora picked up one of the cloths—a particularly large one—and thrust it toward me.

"Wrap this around you and stand over there," she said, pointing to the far-most corner of the room.

I had not the slightest notion of disobeying her. I would do anything to lessen the shame I felt standing there naked, so I grabbed the cloth and was thankful to see how large it was. I folded it around me so that nothing, save my head, was visible, and retreated to the corner.

She shouted for Grimani, and when he didn't come immediately, she grumbled and swore to herself and shouted again, stretching his name out in a taut string of anger. "Grimaaani!"

He appeared in the doorway, breathing hard, and I knew he'd responded at her first call and came to her as quickly as he could. He carried two large wooden pails full of steaming water.

The signora didn't speak to him, didn't even look at him. She merely clapped her hands, and he hurried to pour one of the pails of water into the vat, then set the second one next to it and hurried out of the room.

"Come!" The signora's tone was so sharp I was afraid not to obey her. I walked toward her, taking short little steps because of the way the cloth was wrapped so tightly around me. When I was next to her with only the steaming vat between us, I stopped, still clutching the edges of my wrap as tightly as I could.

She spoke one word, and it was full of impatience. "Well?"

I didn't know what she meant and could only stare at her.

"Get in!"

Get in? Did she mean for me to get into the vat with the steaming water? Was she hoping to scald my skin the way we scalded the skin of chickens and ducks in order to loosen the feathers to butcher them? I wasn't about to do such a thing.

"Ah!" she said, throwing both hands up. *"Idiòta!"* Grabbing the hand I was using to hold the wrap around me, she thrust it into the water while the wrap fell to the floor. The water was not scalding, but was only a little more than comfortably warm.

"Get in!" she said again.

I wasn't sure how she meant for me to do that. The only baths I could remember taking were in the stream near our cottage, a small tributary of the Potenza River. My mother had instructed me to crawl into the stream and then submerge myself before rubbing myself with the tallow soap. This vat was not long enough to submerge my entire body, but I did the best I could. I lifted one leg and placed it knee-down in the vat, then pulled the other leg in, so that I was crouching in the water on my knees.

This made the signora angry for some reason I couldn't fathom. She swatted me hard on my buttocks and at the same time pushed me down so that I lay sideways in the vat with my knees almost to my chin. She gave a disgusted grunt and threw the lump of soap at me.

"Sit up and bathe!" she said.

I sat up with my knees bent and rubbed the soap over my body as my mother had taught me. This seemed to satisfy the signora to some extent, but she kept instructing me to rub harder, and finally handed me a rough stone and told me to rub it on my elbows, knees, and the knuckles of my hands. I was quite exhausted and felt like a skinned hare when she finally picked up the second pail of water and poured it over me, including my head. The water had cooled considerably, and the shock of that cool temperature made me cry out. The signora ignored me and worked some of the soap into my hair.

If she had used just a little less pressure, her massaging of my head might have been a pleasant experience. As it was, her fingers dug into my scalp, so that by the time she finally rinsed the soap away, my head was throbbing. It seemed as if an eternity had passed by the time I was finally allowed to climb out of the vat and once again wrap my shivering body in the large cloth.

The signora paid no attention to my discomfort. Instead she turned away from me toward a chest and pulled from it several articles of clothing, the likes of which I'd never seen, including a thin linen garment as white as goose down. I thought first it was a dress of some sort. I've since learned the garment is called a shift and is meant to be worn under a dress. She also had long hose, a pair of soft leather shoes, a set of very light blue brocade sleeves, and an overgown of what I later learned was called damask in the color of pale sunshine.

Next she proceeded to dress me in these fine garments; then she dried my hair with one of the cloths and dressed it with ribbons intertwined around my head. She pulled out a small tin box and opened it to reveal a fine red powder.

"Moisten your lips with your tongue," she commanded.

I obeyed her, and she used a small brush to apply the powder to my lips and then to a spot on each of my cheeks. After that she led me to a looking glass. I knew what it was because I'd seen one in the marketplace about a year before. It is supposed to show a person an image of herself. The one I stood before now did not show a true image. Not only were there the same waves and ripples I saw when I tried to look at my reflection in the stream, but the image thrown back at me by this glass was not me at all, although the dress, except for the ripples, was the same. The face could not have been mine. It was far too grown-up and beautiful.

The signora was smiling, as if she'd played some clever trick on me. She took my arm and led me toward the door.

"Come with me," she said. "But don't say anything except, 'Yes, master,' and, 'No, master.' "

It was not easy for me to walk down the stairs, because the skirt was exceptionally heavy and the shift kept twisting around my legs. At least the shoes were comfortable. I felt almost as if I were barefooted. Until then, the only time I'd worn shoes was in winter, and they were made of wood and were much heavier and more uncomfortable than the shoes the signora gave me.

She made me wait in the front hall while she opened the door and stepped into a side room and spoke to Master Vasari. In a little while she motioned with a wave of her hand that I should enter. I walked into the room and saw him sitting at a long table with some documents scattered around. He was holding a stylus in his hand. As soon as I entered, he laid the stylus down and looked at me for what seemed a very long time before he smiled broadly.

Finally he spoke in a low voice. *"Bella! Bella!"* And then louder to the signora, *"Eccellénte, Lorenzia, tu ès mago!"*

The signora smiled and nodded without even so much as a *gràzie* for the compliment he'd just given her.

Without taking his eyes off of me, he spoke to her again. "Leave us, Lorenzia."

"Leave you?" The signora sounded shocked. "Of course not. It's not proper for the two of you—"

"I said leave us." His voice had grown louder.

"Dominico, you will not speak to me that way. I am your mother's sister; remember that. And remember that you asked me to act as chaperone until—"

"You are here because you have nowhere else to go, Lorenzia. You are here at my pleasure. I can ask you to leave at any time. Now do as I say."

The signora was silent a moment before she bowed and mumbled, "Yes, my nephew," and quickly left the room.

As soon as the door closed, Master Vasari signaled me with a wave of his hand to come closer. I moved toward him, but my steps were slow and reluctant. I stopped in front of him with the table between us. He stood and walked around the table to take my hand and kiss it.

"I knew you were beautiful, but I had no idea you could be

this lovely." He ran his hand over the fine sleeves I wore and then across the front of my breasts. As soon as he did that, I took a step backward, away from him. That seemed to amuse him, and he laughed softly and pulled me closer to him, kissing me on the mouth. He was holding me so close, I found it impossible to move away. "Yes," he said, when he had finally let me go. "You are more beautiful than any other woman in San Severino. My friends will curdle with envy when they see you."

"You bought me only to make your friends envious?" I asked.

"Oh, you can speak," he said, studying me again with his intense gaze. "I bought you for whatever reason I decide." He pulled me close to him again and kissed me roughly, moving his hands over my body, even between my legs, as much as my dress would allow. I struggled to get away, but he only pulled me closer and kissed me again.

Suddenly he pushed me away as if something had angered him. "Go! Go, damn you." He gave me a shove and returned to his chair behind the table. I hurried out of the room as quickly as possible. Once I was in the hallway again, I leaned against the door and sobbed. I stopped and sucked in my breath with a screech when I saw Lorenzia appearing out of the shadows. It was as if she had materialized out of nowhere. Maybe she really was a *mago*, a magician, as Master Vasari had suggested.

"Save your tears," she said in her harsh voice. "They'll do no good anyway. He'll do as he wishes with you." She took my arm and led me up the stairs to the room where I'd had my bath. "Wait in here," she said. "He'll summon you if he wants you."

She left then, and when I tried to open the door I found that she had locked it from the outside. There was nothing for me to do except pace the floor and glance out the open shutters now and then to the trees in the garden below me. There was no one down there in that garden. Nothing for me to see except the treetops. I could hear birds, but only occasionally could I see one.

I longed for something to do—perhaps spinning or sewing or even feeding swine. But I could do none of that. In a little while I lay down on the bed and heard the straw of the mattress breaking and shifting beneath me. That made me think of the straw I'd lain in with Augustino. I wanted to cry, but it seemed I had no more tears. I had only my loneliness and my fear.

I don't know when I fell asleep, but when I awoke to the sound of a key in the lock, I could see that the sun had sunk low on the horizon and shadows marked the ground in the courtyard. I sat up in bed.

"Who's there?" I asked just as Grimani opened the door and stepped into my room holding a tray in his hands.

"Your supper, signorina." He spoke without looking at me and set the tray on the table next to my bed. He turned to leave without another word, but I called him back.

"Grimani! Wait!"

54

He halted and turned toward me, reluctantly, I thought, and he kept his head down and wouldn't look at me.

"How long have you lived here?"

"Five years, signorina." His voice was so quiet I could hardly hear him.

"What's it like? Living here, I mean?"

He glanced up at me for the first time and wore a surprised look, but he didn't speak.

I tried to prompt him. "Well, do you like it?"

After a long pause he spoke. "Like it? What does it matter? I'm a servant. I have no choice."

I realized then how foolish I'd been. My question would have been like someone asking me if I liked being the daughter of a peasant and spending my life in the fields. It would have never occurred to me what I liked or didn't like if I hadn't had my life uprooted and been forced into such alien circumstances.

"Of course," I said, embarrassed. "I guess what I really want to know is . . . well, what's he like?"

The way he looked at me made me think he might not have understood me. Finally he shrugged and said in his quiet voice, "He pays me a little and don't beat me too often. I guess it could be worse." He turned around and walked quickly to the door, but just before he reached it he turned back to me. "I know you're scared," he said. "You being fresh from the fields and nothing but a child, at that. But don't worry. You'll be his wife, not his servant. He'll most likely treat you fine if you minds your ways."

"But tell me how I—"

"I mustn't be talking to you, signorina. I'm in for a thrashing if he finds out."

With that he was gone, and I was once again left to be alone in my luxurious bedroom. I looked at the contents of the tray for the first time. What I saw was a meal such as I never imagined. There was a piece of roasted meat covered with a brown sauce, a dish of peas and onions in a white sauce, a loaf of dark bread with olive oil, and a plate of nuts and almonds. I thought I could never eat such a feast, but I did at least want to taste it. The meat had such a wonderful flavor I thought it might have been roasted in heaven, and the peas and onions were equally as good. I dipped my fingers into the sauces several times and licked them with pleasure. I sampled the almonds and dates, too, although at the time I didn't know what they were called. However, dates have, ever since that day, been my favorite food.

The meal amused me for a short time, but in a little while I grew so lonely I might have gone mad if I hadn't found my way to the window again. I leaned out, making a game out of trying to count the number of different birdsongs I heard. I also found I could stand on the ledge beneath my window and place bread crumbs there to coax a few birds to come near me. I don't know how long I'd been out on that ledge when I heard a noise at my door. There was barely time for me to scramble back into the room before the door opened. This time it was Lorenzia who entered.

Without looking at me or speaking to me, she picked up the tray Grimani had brought me, and started for the door.

"Signora!" I said. She ignored me, so I tried something else. "Lorenzia!"

When she turned around, I saw that her face had gone sour. "What did you call me?"

"Lorenzia, signora. You didn't seem to know I was speaking to you when I—"

"You will never address me that way again. You will call me signora or Signora Lorenzia."

Her tone was biting, but since the dressing-down she'd received from Master Vasari, I was a little less afraid of her. "Of course, signora. I only wanted to make certain of exactly who you are. You are Master Vasari's aunt?"

She pushed her very prominent nose a little higher into the air and said, "I am the sister of Dominico Vasari's deceased mother. I am his only living relative, and he asked me to live with him and to be the mistress of his house. That is what I am, and that is what I shall always be."

It was clear to me now that she was jealous of me. She feared I was going to usurp her role as mistress of the house. So did that mean she was also afraid of me? I was confused by this unexpected revelation and wasn't quite sure how I should react. When I saw she was about to leave again, I called her back.

"Signora . . ." To speak to her again was a bold move on my part and certainly not something I would have ordinarily done. I'm not certain whether it was my desperation or my newfound power that prompted me to do such a thing. "Signora, tell me, when am I to be married?"

She gave me another one of those looks that made me feel as if she smelled something unpleasant. "Certainly not for a while," she said. "Dominico doesn't want to be embarrassed by you, and turning you into something presentable won't happen overnight—if ever."

She left, slamming the door behind her, and I was once again alone in my room. I went to the window again and sat on the ledge, dangling my feet outside. The birds had all found their nests for the night, and I soon grew tired of the silence. In a little while I removed my fine new dress and fell asleep on the luxurious bed, wearing only my linen shift.

I slept fitfully, perhaps partly because I'd slept so much during the day, but also because I feared Master Vasari would come into my room to take advantage of me. He didn't come, for which I was both surprised and grateful. I'm certain it was he I heard pacing the hallway during the night. It was not the light steps of a woman I heard, and Grimani would not have been in that part of the house during the night.

By first light I was awake. I was standing at the window,

still in my shift, and contemplating my escape when someone knocked on the door and called out, "Breakfast." I had decided my escape would be made in my shift, since it was easier to move in it, and I would take one of the coverlets from the bed to wear as a robe so I would not look immodest.

I expected to see Lorenzia come in with my tray, since it was a woman's voice I'd heard. The person who entered, however, was not Lorenzia, but a younger woman who was very thin and frail.

"*Buòn giorno*, signorina. Here is your breakfast." She coughed, a wet, rattling sound, and set a tray on the table at the side of the bed. The tray held a small loaf of bread and a little bowl of olive oil. I could hardly believe my good fortune to be served olive oil two meals in a row. The young woman stepped back from the table and folded her hands in front of her. "I am Fausta." She coughed again. "I am to be your servant. I was not able to come to you until today. For that I ask your forgiveness, and I pray that the master will forgive me as well. I couldn't help not being here, my lady. I was ill."

"I'm sorry you were ill. I'm certain Master Vasari will understand that."

"Ha!" Fausta said. "He shows his understanding with a strong leather strap. But he wouldn't dare hit me too hard or send me out to the street, either. Where else would he find a girl to work as cheap as . . ."

She started coughing again and continued until she was

red and puffy in the face. "The signora says . . . she says I must . . ."

It took her several minutes to tell me that Signora Lorenzia had instructed her to help me dress. I was glad that Fausta stayed to help me, since I wasn't certain how to get the dress and the sleeves on right. I certainly had no idea of how to arrange my hair, but Fausta did an even better job than Lorenzia had.

"Your hair is lovely, my lady," she said when she had finished. "Is this the style you are accustomed to? The one your former hairdresser made for you?"

I laughed. "The style I am accustomed to is to have my hair full of straw from the fields."

She gave me a curious look.

"I am a peasant from the fields of the Duke of Angeni. Surely you must have known that."

"I'd heard gossip from Grimani, maybe, but why would I believe him?"

It was then that I knew she must have known my background all along, but since it would not be proper for her to ask me directly, she'd been clever enough to find another way to get the confirmation.

"I don't belong here," I said. "And I don't like it, either. I will leave as soon as I . . ." Immediately I was afraid that I'd said too much. Perhaps Fausta was spying. Perhaps she'd been ordered to report my words back to the master.

She laughed when she saw my face. "Don't worry; I won't say a word. Truth is, if I could find a better place, I'd leave myself. But we're both trapped here, because the worst truth is, we'd both end up selling our bodies if we left."

Her words both shocked and frightened me. She must have seen that on my face as well, because she reached one of her frail hands to pat my arm before she turned away, coughing once again as she left the room.

After she left I sat in my room, waiting for whatever would happen to me next. I sat sometimes on the bed and sometimes on an uncomfortable bench near the fireplace. No one came. No one, that is, except Fausta, who brought me another meal, this time of meat and porridge. She stayed a little while to talk, to tell me about the cook, whose name was Rufina, who had been a peasant herself, and how Grimani grew angry when she tried to tell him how to do his work. She made me laugh when she described their bantering, and for a little while I forgot about wanting to run away.

I couldn't forget her words about what would happen to me if I left, but a part of me still wanted to leave, and I tried to convince myself that I would have to endure only a little while longer before I found a way.

Since Fausta wasn't there to keep me company, I tried going back to the window to count the bird sounds, but my ability with numbers was limited, and I was unable to count high enough. So I grew bored.

When Fausta came back the next morning with another breakfast, I asked, "When will I be allowed out of my room?" She at least gave me a reply if not an answer.

"How should I know a thing such as that? I know nothing but the kitchen and the chamber pots." She spoke in such a sullen way that I was reluctant to ask her another time. She stared at me for a moment, then gave me a weak smile. "Don't be so eager to go out into the world, my lady. You're not going to like the master's world much, or his friends either."

"Really? Why not?"

"You'll see soon enough." She glanced over her shoulder. "But mind you don't mention my words to anyone."

I was alone in my room for five more days. Each day I looked forward to Fausta coming, but she came all too infrequently, and, although she stayed as long as she could, her visits were all too brief. With so much time on my hands, it was then that two things happened that would affect my life more than I could have possibly known at the time.

I discovered a way to lower myself into the garden below by walking along the ledge to a heavy, tangled vine I could climb down. And I began to spend long hours in prayer.

Chapter 5

IT DIDN'T TAKE ME long to realize I was not particularly gifted at praying. I tried to remember the prayers the priest had taught all of us, but I found that without his aid and without the entire congregation repeating his words, my memory of the prayers was poor. I did my best to invoke a vision of the Holy Mother or of anything holy, but the best I could do was a slight fuzziness in the distance when I half closed my eyes, or a black spot in the center of a blinding redness when I tried to look at the sun. The frightening thought occurred to me that the black spot could be Satan, so I stopped the practice altogether.

The only thing I could do was to try to talk in long monologues to the Holy Mother, or Saint Mary of Magdala, who the priest told us had at one time been a great sinner and knew the way to redemption. I told both her and the Mother of God about my love for Augustino and confessed what we had done together and asked for forgiveness now that I could not marry him. I told them about my dislike for Master Vasari and Signora Lorenzia and for the dreadful life they, along with my family, had forced upon me.

Neither of them ever answered me. Not one word. I was

becoming a little angry about that until I realized how much better I felt after the long talks. So I decided it may be—although I was not certain about this—that the saints speak to us in ways we don't expect.

I became quite interested in testing the two Marys to try to determine just how they might speak, if they spoke at all, but my experiment was interrupted by a surprise visit.

I had long since stopped expecting Master Vasari to come to my room, so when he did show up, I was quite unprepared. Fausta had been in to take my hair down from its elaborate weaving, and she had helped me into a nightdress. All of that preparation for bed, I might add, seemed completely unnecessary to me at first, since I was used to sleeping in the same clothes I wore daily. However, by the end of the first week I had begun to look forward to the refreshing change and to the nightly hair combing, which I found soothing, and of course to the little talks Fausta and I shared.

I had just gotten into bed and was propped up with two pillows—even one seemed a luxury to me—and I was trying to arrange my thoughts for how I might get my saints to speak to me, but I was having a hard time keeping away memories of how it felt when Augustino made love to me. The door opened, and for a moment I was at first afraid it might be one of the Marys, who would find me touching myself with longing for Augustino, but I soon saw that it was Master Vasari.

"Oh, it's you," I said.

"And whom did you expect? Grimani, perhaps?"

I found it impossible to reply at first, since Grimani was the last person I expected, and because I thought Master Vasari's voice sounded angry. Then when he ripped the covers back to stare at my naked legs, because my nightdress had ridden up almost to my thighs, I was even more frightened. He stared at my legs for a moment until something resembling a smile began to curl his lips. He placed one of his hands on the calf of my left leg and sat down on the bed and shifted his eyes to my face.

Still smiling, he slid his hand up the inside of my thigh and massaged me in my most private spot.

"You're wet!" His voice was a husky whisper. "Who were you thinking of?"

I didn't answer, but he didn't seem to notice.

"It's been a long time," he said. "I was too ill with a headache to come to you for a while, but I think the wait was worth it." He removed his hand from my body and stood up to untie the front laces of his tight-fitting hose. He was fumbling and nervous. "Yes!" he said, freeing his long, stiff member from its confines. "Yes! It has been worth it!"

He fell on top of me while at the same time moving my nightdress up to my waist. "Yes!" he said again. "At long last, I . . ."

He was still on top of me, and I felt him trying to work himself into me, felt his strength slowly dissolve to a soft mound of warm flesh, but still he wouldn't stop trying to force all that softness into me until finally he flung himself off of me with a loud curse. "Damn you! Damn you, you worthless vermin!"

It wasn't clear to me whether it was I he swore at or himself, or perhaps even his soft member. He stood up, scooped up his clothes, and glanced down at me.

"I thought you would be the cure!" he said. "When I first saw you I grew hard as marble. That's why I bought you. But you've failed me just like all the others." With that he turned and left my room, naked except for his short tunic. He slammed the door as he left, and I found that I was holding my breath and didn't release it until I heard the key turn in the lock.

I was so upset I couldn't stop sobbing, and if I hadn't been afraid of losing my immortal soul, I would have railed out at the two Marys, and God as well, for not showing up when I needed them. Of course, it occurred to me that perhaps they *had* intervened, since Master Vasari's attempt to assault me wasn't successful. Still, I couldn't help thinking that if I were a saint I would have stepped in much earlier. I did my best to comfort myself that at least he'd been unable to complete the assault, and after a while I was able to sleep.

My rest was cut short, however, when Fausta appeared in my room much earlier than usual with my breakfast tray. She set the tray on the table in the same manner she always did, but instead of her usual, "Good morning, signorina," she mumbled something under her breath.

I glanced at her with my sleep-fogged eyes. "What did you say?"

She didn't answer immediately, and for the first time I noticed that her face was creased with a worried look.

I tried again. "Is something wrong?"

This time she answered in a whisper and with a glance toward the door, as if she were afraid someone might be listening. "I wanted to get here early, before you . . ." She signaled toward the window with her head and gave one of her wheezy coughs.

I was shocked to realize she obviously knew I'd found a way to escape my room to the garden below. If she knew, who else might know? And what might my punishment be? I started to speak. "How did you—"

"Shhh!" she said, glancing at the door again. "The signora will be up soon. Just eat your breakfast." With that she hurried out of the room, leaving me to dress myself.

It was still a challenge to me to manage all of the various garments I was expected to wear, but I did get the shift and the overdress on, although I felt oddly dizzy and unsettled by the time it was accomplished. The sleeves were too difficult, so I left them off and tried to arrange my hair. I had no skill with weaving ribbons into my hair, and all I could do was comb it. That alone was a pleasure for me. We had only one comb at home, and it had several broken teeth. Each member of the family used it, and it was not unusual for me to have to leave for my work in the field before I got my turn. Now that I had a comb for myself, I felt a guilty pleasure at using it. Guilty because, as everyone knows, vanity is a sin.

I put the comb aside to assuage my guilt and turned to my breakfast of bread and olive oil with a few grapes. It was a sumptuous breakfast, one that I never knew was possible even to dream of until I came here. Now I had it every single morning. It seemed that all the rich and plentiful food I'd been served in the week I'd been there was not setting well with me. I could hardly stand to look at the food without feeling sick, although my stomach felt empty.

To stop the gnawing feeling, I did manage to eat a small piece of the crust of the bread, without the olive oil and without the grapes. I was still chewing when Signora Lorenzia entered my room.

"*Santa Madre!*" she said, rolling her eyes. "Who dressed you? That worthless Fausta?"

"No, signora, I dressed myself."

She paid no attention. I'm not sure she even heard me. She went on exclaiming to herself as if I'd committed a terrible crime of some sort. "You look ridiculous! I'm sure you're beyond anything Fausta could manage. I can see that I have my work cut out for me. Why, I've half a mind to march you down to Dominico so he can see for himself, and mind you, I would, were he not in one of his foul moods. Another headache, I suppose. Ugh! You have crumbs all over your mouth. Put it down! You've had enough."

I put the bread crust aside, although I'd had only two or three bites. It had, at least, made me feel a little better. Signora Lorenzia had a way of making me lose my appetite anyway.

"Come here!" She spoke in her angry, commanding voice. "Dominico wants me to instruct you. It will not be easy. I hope he realizes that."

I approached her as she had bidden me, but I was cautious because I didn't know what to expect. "Instruct me?" I asked in my quiet, timid voice. In spite of my uneasiness, I was a little excited, thinking perhaps I would be taught to read or to play a musical instrument, as some grand ladies were taught. "In what will you instruct me?"

That last question made Signora Lorenzia laugh, but it was a harsh laugh. "I shall have to instruct you in everything." She put one of my sleeves in place and gave it such a hard tug it almost made me fall. "You are utterly ignorant." Another hard tug. "There is nothing you know. Now sit there." She pointed to a bench near the fireplace. "And I'll try to do something with your hair."

The tugs she made on my sleeves were nothing compared to the hard pulls and yanks she made at my hair. I felt as if my very head might be bleeding by the time she finished, but I was determined not to make a sound.

At last she stopped pulling at my hair and told me to stand. "I'm going to teach you to walk," she said.

I looked at her, surprised and not sure how to respond. In fact, I wasn't certain that I'd heard her correctly, since I already knew how to walk.

"You walk like a peasant," she said. "Long steps, your back straight as if you had something balanced on your head. Pffft!" She added the last as if she had a need to spit out the vileness in her mouth after uttering words about me. "Walk like this," she said, making her way across the room with mincing steps, her right arm bent at the elbow and her wrist limp.

I tried, but I tripped on the hem of my skirt and fell to the floor, which made her angry. I was angry, too, because I scraped both of my knees, but I didn't tell her. She worked and worked on teaching me to walk, until she finally gave up when Fausta came in with the noon meal for both of us.

Since I had eaten very little that morning, I was hungry, and as soon as the trays were on the table I helped myself to some of the roasted meat in the same wonderful brown sauce I'd had before. I hadn't even gotten the first morsel to my mouth before Signora Lorenzia yelled at me.

"Pig! Pig! You eat like a pig! You *do not* pick up the food with your fingers!"

Again I was puzzled. Why was she saying I ate like a pig because I picked up the food with my fingers? I happened to know quite a lot about pigs, and I was certain they did not pick

up food with fingers. And anyway, how else was a person supposed to eat? Surely she wasn't suggesting I put my face in the
plate and eat like an animal?

"This!" she said, waving the strange wooden-handled
spoon that always accompanied my meals. She waved it so
close to my nose, I was afraid she would hit me. I backed away
from her, but that made her angry, too. In fact, it seemed *everything* made her angry. She picked up the cloth that also always
accompanied my meals and threw it at me. By this time I had
figured out that it was a cloth for wiping my hands after I ate,
which I did this time, although I was by no means finished.

"Like this," she said, using the spoon to scoop up some of
the food on her plate and bring it to her mouth. I'd seen ladles
and spoons before, but they were for dipping food out of a pot,
not for an individual to use for eating. She produced a knife
from a fold in her skirt and used it to cut the meat into smaller
pieces. Of course, I'd seen a knife as well, since we used them
at home for butchering. I was taken completely by surprise
when she produced another knife from her pocket and told me
it was to be mine and that I must never lose it.

I was quite exhausted by the time she stopped instructing
me. We had practiced walking and eating and even talking. She
said I was no better at that than I was at anything else. She
complained that I spoke like an ignorant peasant. If I hadn't
been so exhausted, I might have asked how she expected me to
speak if not like what I was.

I was grateful for the opportunity to fall into bed, and I was far too tired for conversations with any saints. My reprieve was all too short, since she was back early the next morning in time to make certain I ate my breakfast properly. I was so upset, I had to excuse myself and throw up in the chamber pot. The lessons went on for days, but at least she didn't come early every morning. I sensed it was because she was becoming as weary as I was of the grueling lessons.

I had begun to feel tired almost all of the time, and it seemed I was frequently having to use the chamber pot to throw up the contents of my stomach, which made me worry. An even greater worry was that it was past the phase of the moon during which I always had my menses, and my breasts had become tender and swollen.

What would happen to me? If Master Vasari learned I was pregnant—and of course he would, eventually—would he send me back to my family? That would be the best of all possible things that could come to pass. Augustino and I could marry, just as we'd planned to do all along, and I would not have to bear a child in shame. I pushed aside the memory of his attitude when I left, as well as the fact that he had made no attempt to rescue me. I would not allow the thought I'd come to have at times to stay in my mind—the thought that perhaps I didn't really wish to be married to him at all. I pushed all of that aside, because being transported back to my old life, no matter how unsatisfactory, would be for the best. When Master

Vasari learned I was with child, he could just as easily turn me out on the streets in a city where I would not know how to take care of myself.

He hadn't returned to bother me in several days, and I tried to be grateful for that. However, I found that, because of the way I felt, it was difficult for me to feel grateful for anything. Also, I'd become so angry with my inept saints that I no longer even tried to speak to either of them.

I don't know how long I might have wallowed in my misery if Lorenzia hadn't come to me with yet another surprise.

She burst into the room early one evening, as usual without knocking, and began talking as soon as she entered. "He wants you ready within an hour. I just hope he understands my disadvantage at having such a poor specimen to work with. Impossible!" She tossed a dress on my bed and shouted over her shoulder, "Fausta!" She went to the chest in the corner near the mirror and pulled out the comb and ribbons, muttering to herself. It was difficult for me to understand all of her words, but I could hear enough to know she was still complaining about how difficult her job of trying to refine me had been.

"Fausta!" she called again, louder this time. She turned to me. "Don't just stand there like a fool. Take off your clothes." By then Fausta had come. She was out of breath, as if she'd been running. Signora Lorenzia attacked her immediately. "What took you so long? Can't you learn to come when I call? Go on, help the poor fool. Dominico is taking her out tonight to meet his friends. Hurry! Hurry! Why do I have to tell you everything twice?" She turned back to me. "Look at you! Your face is a ghastly color! I'm supposed to work miracles and make you beautiful?"

Fausta helped me strip down to my shift, then helped me into the gown the signora had tossed on the bed. It was even more beautiful than the one I'd been wearing since I had arrived. This one was a lovely silk so pale it was almost white, with close-fitting sleeves and a low, rounded neckline. The signora pulled and stretched and fluffed it until it met her satisfaction, then tied the waist with a girdle of blue silk.

Fausta combed and arranged my hair and tied a jewel-encrusted ribbon around the sculpted mass. Signora Lorenzia, once again grumbling about my pallid skin, produced her tin box of red clay dust and applied a spot on each side of my face as well as my lips. The last thing she did was take my spoon and knife from the chest and hand them to me.

"See that you use them properly!" she said.

She had been so tense and agitated the entire time she was dressing me that I actually felt quite exhausted by the time she finished and pulled me, none too gently, out of my room and down the stairs to where Master Vasari was waiting in the hall.

"Good," he said when he saw me. "You've done it again, Lorenzia." There was none of his effusiveness about how beautiful I was this time. There was not even a smile. He himself was dressed in a short brocaded tunic with long strips of cloth hanging from the elbows in the fashion of gentlemen, and a short cape that came only to his elbows. His shoes were slightly raised at the heel and were adorned with buckles of the shiniest metal I'd ever seen. He held a lightweight cloak, which he draped over my shoulders, then took my arm as he led me out the door and into the courtyard.

"It's time you met my friends," he said as he ushered me through the gate and onto the street. "We couldn't keep you hidden forever. People would start to talk, but I couldn't present you the way you were."

There was no hint of affection in his voice. In fact, it was almost as if he weren't talking to me at all, but to himself. After we'd walked a short distance along the street, lined with other large houses partially hidden behind courtyards, he stopped in front of one of them and turned me around, holding my forearms as if he wanted to make certain I knew he was addressing me this time.

"We're going inside to attend a banquet in honor of the marriage of the son of Urbino, the wine merchant. Speak as little as possible, and mind you don't use your fingers to eat. Do you understand?"

I nodded. "Yes, Master Vasari."

A scowl marred his handsome face. "Henceforth you will call me Dominico."

"Dominico," I said, trying it out.

He nodded and led me to the courtyard gate. As we drew

closer to the open door I could hear loud voices and the sound of laughter, and I could see men and women dressed in fine clothes lounging around a long table, and some milling around talking to the other guests. It looked as if it was a merry party. Still, I found myself dreading to step inside.

Just as we entered, a plump woman dressed in blue silk greeted us. Or at least she greeted Dominico.

"Dominico!" She wrapped her arms around him. "I was beginning to worry that you wouldn't be here. It's been so long since we've seen you. You work far, far too hard, my dear, but you are, of course, as handsome as ever." She continued gushing over him for a while before she turned to me. "Oh, yes, this must be the one we've heard about. Why have you kept her hidden? Or should I ask?" She winked at him. "I hope for the sake of your immortal soul that you haven't been naughty with her." She laughed, as if to say she wasn't really worried about his immortal soul at all.

"This is Margherita, my betrothed." Dominico held my arm in a proprietary manner. "Margherita, our hostess, Madame Urbino."

I managed a polite little nod of my head in the manner the signora had taught me while Madame Urbino inspected me.

"Young," she said, her eyes moving from my head to my feet. She winked at Dominico again. "And beautiful, just as you said." She took Dominico's arm and led him toward the table. "Ah, Dominico, you are quite the rake, aren't you?" She turned back to me. "Come along, child; you must meet his friends."

I followed her to the table and sat on the bench next to Dominico as she instructed me to do. Several people got up from their seats at the table and came to us.

"So you've finally brought her out!" one man said, slapping Dominico on the back and looking me up and down just as Madame Urbino had done. "Selfish of you to keep her to yourself. She's charming."

Others said similar things, but nothing they said was addressed to me. I had begun to feel, again, like an animal taken to the market for others to appraise. Dominico was enjoying it. He smiled broadly as everyone congratulated him on having found such a prize heifer. While I sat there and endured their remarks, I noticed that others at the table had taken spoons and knives from small bags. They were dipping the spoons into various large dishes on the table, eating, and dipping again. It was then that I understood why Signora Lorenzia had thrust my own spoon and knife into my hand. I had no desire to use the spoon to dip into the dishes, however. Grease floated on top of one of the meat dishes, which, although I craved grease in times of famine, looked unappetizing to me now.

At one point Dominico turned to me and ordered me to eat. I dipped my spoon into the dish and took a small taste of something. That didn't satisfy him, though. He used his own spoon to feed me several mouthfuls while those around us cooed about how attentive he was. And he was attentive, I must admit, not only feeding me but making certain my wineglass was filled and occasionally kissing my hand or brushing his lips across my cheek. When a servant brought quartered roasted pigeons on long slices of trenched bread, he used his own knife to cut morsels for me, which wouldn't have been necessary, since I'm quite adept with a knife.

I was glad when the meal was finally over and all of the toasts had been drunk to the Urbino family's betrothed son. I had managed to get through the meal doing just as Lorenzia had taught me, using my spoon instead of my fingers and saying no more than, "Yes, thank you," or "No, thank you." I hoped, once the toasts were over, that we would be able to go home, since the greasy food I'd eaten had begun to make me feel sickened, and the wine was giving me a headache.

It was not to be. After the meal the guests milled around and gathered in small conversation groups. Dominico was talking to a group of men about Guelphs and Ghibellines. I had no idea what those things were, except that I assumed from the conversation that they must be groups of people whose ideas regarding the government differed.

While they were talking, three young women walked up to me to admire my dress. I smiled and thanked them for the compliment, as I'd been taught. The list of words and phrases the signora had approved for me was short, and I quickly ran through them, leaving me with nothing to say. For that reason

I hoped the young women would move on to someone else. They didn't.

"So you're to be his wife," one of them said. She had thick dark hair that reminded me of my mother's and beautiful skin and eyes. "What did you do to capture him that the rest of us couldn't do?"

"Capture him?" I was nervous, since there was nothing on the approved list I could use to reply to that. Besides, my dinner was now trying to work its way back to my throat.

The woman laughed. "Are you really so naive, or are you just being coy? I suspect you know all of the tricks."

"I know of no tricks," I said.

"Then let me teach you." That made all of the women laugh.

"We all need a trick or two at times," said a woman with a plain face and an elaborate gown.

"So true," said the third. "That thing between a man's legs that he prizes so needs only the trick of a little stroking to produce a new gown or another servant."

Everyone laughed even harder until one of them, the beautiful one, gave me a look of concern or curiosity, I wasn't certain which. "Your face has turned an odd shade of green," she said.

"I . . . I think I'm going to . . ." And then it was too late. The greasy beef and fattened pigeon did not stay down. Everyone in the room witnessed its reappearance, including Dominico.

Chapter 6

AFTER THAT DISASTER, it seemed to me that everything happened at once. I saw the three women back away from me, heard expressions of alarm, heard laughter and shouting, and knew that someone who must have been a servant rushed toward me with a pail of water and a towel.

I also saw the angry look on Dominico's face. With a cruel gesture he brushed aside the hand of some gentleman who, it appeared, was offering sympathy. Someone, an older woman, I think, put an arm around my shoulder, and I suddenly became even more aware of rude laughter. I felt my face grow hot from embarrassment and tried to resist when I realized the woman was leading me toward Dominico. I didn't want to be by his side. All I wanted was to disappear somehow.

The beautiful woman I'd just spoken with was next to him, and I heard her voice again.

"Dominico! I knew it! I knew you wouldn't wait for a ceremony before you plowed your new field." She laughed, and Dominico managed a smile.

"Take her home," the kind woman who had led me to him said. "Put the poor child to bed."

"It appears he may have already done that," someone said, making everyone laugh.

"You devil," one of the men said. To my surprise I realized by the look on his face that the words were meant as a compliment. They all knew I was with child and thought it was Dominico's.

Dominico had lost his scowl, and took my hand to pull me toward him. "If you'll excuse us, I will take her to bed—I mean I'll take her home now." There was more laughter as Dominico raised a hand to bid good-bye to the young Urbino, whose betrothal we were celebrating. "May your bed be as warm as mine," he said as we moved toward the door.

We left amidst bawdy laughter and hoots.

Dominico led me out with his arm over my shoulder in a protective and gentle gesture. As soon as we passed through the courtyard gates and were on the street, his manner changed abruptly and he pushed me away, almost causing me to fall.

"I told you not to embarrass me!" His voice was hard and cold.

I said nothing in reply. Certainly it was obvious, without my saying it, that I hadn't embarrassed him on purpose. My silence angered him.

"Have you nothing to say for yourself? Don't you realize everyone in the place thinks you're pregnant? Flattering as that is to me, don't you realize how it will make a fool of me once everyone realizes that it's only that your peasant's stomach can't digest such rich . . ." He stopped talking and grabbed my arm again, giving me a rough jerk that forced me to look at him. "My God!" he said, realizing the truth at last. He hit me hard across the face, so hard it made me stagger, and I would have fallen had he not still been holding my arm. "Whore!" he said. "You filthy whore! You've got some plowman's bastard on you."

He said no more the rest of the way home, but he kept his grip on my arm, pulling me along roughly and walking at such a pace it was hard for me to keep up. I was too frightened to speak, too afraid of what he would do to me when we arrived at his house. When we reached the front door he flung me inside, and this time I did fall to the floor. He pulled me to my feet and pushed me toward the stairs, still not speaking to me. I hurried up to my room, not daring to look back. Behind me I heard the door to his downstairs office open and then slam behind him.

Alone in my room, I was grateful for the darkness and for the fact that no one came in to help me undress. I could do that myself well enough. I untied the uncomfortably tight silk girdle from my waist and sat down on my bed with my head in my hands, afraid once again of what might happen to me. I sat for a long time before I finally stood and pulled my dress off over my head, preparing for bed and hoping that sleep would numb my fears.

I was standing in the darkness, dressed only in my shift

and turning back the coverlet on the bed, when I heard the all-too-familiar twist of the key in the lock of my door. I stood motionless and prayed that it would be Fausta. She was the only one I wanted to talk to.

It was Dominico who stood in the doorway, his face illuminated and distorted by the light of the candle he held in his hand. He had removed his short cape as well as the long strips of material that attached to his elbows and marked his status of wealth and standing. My breath caught in my throat, and my heart was trying to tear itself out of my chest.

"Margherita." His voice was eerie and calm as he advanced toward me, still holding the candle. He set the candle on the table near my bed and looked at me, saying nothing for several seconds. I was completely unable to speak and so frightened I felt as if I might faint. He said my name again: "Margherita." He laughed. The laugh was soft and cruel.

"Everyone thinks it's my bastard." Still with that disturbing quietness to his voice. He took a step toward me. I tried to back away, but I bumped into the edge of the bed. "And it is my bastard, isn't it?" He took another step. I was still too afraid to speak. He grabbed me, holding both arms at the top, near my shoulders, and shook me. "Isn't it?" His voice was louder and angrier.

I didn't know what to say at first. If I agreed with him, would he hit me for lying? If I told the truth, would he strike me for what I'd done? He shook me again, so hard it made my head ache, and my eyes felt as if they would fall from their sockets.

"Yes," I said, thinking it best to humor him. "Yes, it's yours."

It worked. He dropped my arms from his hard grip. "That's what you will tell everyone," he said.

He hit me on my face, this time with such force it knocked me onto the bed. He pulled me up to a sitting position and hit me again. I tasted blood and felt some of it trickling down my throat. My right eye had begun to throb.

"That's only a sample of what will happen to you if you say the bastard's not mine." He looked at me a moment while shadows from the flickering candle played with his handsome face, shaping it into something vile. "Now get up!" he said. "And do something about that bloody lip. We'll be announcing the wedding soon. Everyone will expect a quick wedding, given your condition, and you'll want to look your best under your virgin's veil." He said the last with a sneer and turned and left the room.

Fausta came to my room earlier than usual the next morning, and she had no breakfast tray. I was fully dressed and standing next to the window staring at the garden below. I turned around to look at her when she entered.

"Master Vasari says you are to break your fast with him in the . . ." She stopped talking and stared at my face. I had no doubt that the story of the night before was revealed there, because my eye throbbed and my lip, which had turned my pillow bloody, still hurt. I had made up my mind during the night to escape as soon as it was light enough. Whatever dreadful fate awaited me was better than staying in Dominico's house, I thought. I still had no clear plan of how to get out of the garden. The only way to enter or exit was through the house.

"Mistress, your face!" Fausta said when she recovered her voice. "Did he . . ." She gave a quick glance over her shoulder, as if to make sure no one was listening. She walked to the door and closed it and turned toward me. "Did he do that?"

I nodded. Although I was accustomed to an occasional light strapping from my father when he thought I was being lazy, he had never hit me in the face, and he had never hit me hard enough to bruise me.

"You stirred his anger somehow." She spoke in a whisper, which made her cough, and she was still glancing over her shoulder. "Tried to bed you, did he?"

I turned away, embarrassed.

Fausta's harsh laugh embarrassed me even more. "Limp as a dead mouse, was it?"

I faced her again, wondering how she knew that, until I saw the look on her face and remembered that she'd said he had beaten her, too.

"Yes, 'tis as I thought," she said. "Some men's fists grow hard when nothing else will. He smites a woman with his pride."

Hearing her speak brought back the memory of the night before. I felt myself grow dizzy, and then my tongue felt thick and my throat tight. I knew I had to find the chamber pot. Fausta stepped out of the way as I hurried to fetch it from under the bed. When I was finished she dampened the corner of a towel in my water bowl and wiped my face. Just as she finished she pulled down the front of my dress with a sudden jerk.

"Ah, yes," she said, looking at my exposed breasts. "The nipples grow dark and the stomach grows green. You'd do well to get to the church to say your vows with the master as soon as possible, before he finds out."

"He knows," I said, pulling my dress aright. "God has forsaken me." I know I sounded full of self-pity, but at least I managed not to cry.

"*Sì*, and the devil has forsaken you as well. He stays around only for the merriment of it while the seed is planted. I know, for I've seen it happen to more than one of us."

"I must leave," I said, and immediately regretted it. I feared that Fausta had seduced me with her friendliness, because, in truth, she had nothing to gain by befriending me. Betraying me to Dominico would stand her better.

"Leave?" She looked at me as if she thought I might be soft in the head. "Didn't I tell you that you don't leave a place like this? You don't leave a man with the power of Vasari. He would destroy you."

"But . . ."

"But what? You were going to say, 'Who are you to be telling the mistress of the house what to do?' "

"No, I didn't mean—"

"You'd be right, of course. I would be a fool to advise you." She coughed again and placed a handkerchief to her mouth until the paroxysm stopped. "I have everything to lose and nothing to gain by telling you that everyone will think the child is his and that when he sees that, it will feed his pride. I would be even more the fool to tell you to go along with the deception for your own safety and that of your child. I would certainly be a fool to think you would help me if I should give you good advice."

I stared at her a moment, letting it all sink into my mind. Perhaps she did want to help me, and of course she would expect something in return. However, I was about to tell her that going along with the deception wouldn't necessarily protect me. Last night had proved that. I never had the chance. Signora Lorenzia burst into the room.

"Fausta! Fool, I told you to have her ready. What have you been doing? Look at her hair! Well, there's no time to worry about that now." She grabbed my arm and pulled me in front of her. "What is this?" she asked, staring at my bruised face.

I didn't answer, but she must have read the truth in my silence, and it pleased her, for a smile crept across her face. "Go!" She pushed me toward the door. "Don't keep him waiting."

She hurried me along to the dining room and made me sit down on a bench along the side of the table, and then she seated herself in a high-backed chair at the end. We had barely settled ourselves in when Dominico entered. He didn't speak to either of us, but seated himself at the end opposite the signora.

"Good morning, Dominico," Lorenzia said. "I trust you enjoyed yourself at the banquet."

"It was an agreeable evening," he said.

"Perhaps not *entirely* agreeable," she said, and I could see a smug little smile tickling the corners of her mouth. It was obvious she was alluding to whatever disagreement she might be imagining the two of us had.

Dominico's response surprised me. He turned to me, picked up my hand from where I had rested it on the table, and kissed it. "You could not possibly understand, Lorenzia, the manner in which the two of us enjoy ourselves." He spoke without ever taking his eyes off of me. He was looking at me as if we shared some forbidden secret.

At first I couldn't imagine why he was doing that, but I stole a glance at Lorenzia and saw the look of chagrin on her face. Could it possibly be that he was implying I enjoyed his cruelty? That it was a part of our lovemaking? I wanted to scream my denial of such a corrupt thought, but I never had the chance. Dominico immediately launched into a discussion of our wedding plans, ignoring Lorenzia completely.

"I've spoken to the priest, and he's agreed to contact the bishop. It's only fitting that a bishop perform the ceremony for me. We should plan on it taking place in two weeks." His voice was sweet, and he leaned toward me in an attentive manner.

I couldn't respond, couldn't even smile, but it didn't seem to concern him. He went on talking about the guest list and what I should wear and a long list of things that seemed unimportant to me. I couldn't help thinking about my mother and father and Teresa and little Bernardino, just as I had so many times since I'd been in the Vasari house. This time I was remembering how excited Teresa had been about attending the wedding and having a new gown to wear. But Dominico had refused to allow them because they would embarrass him. That made me miss all of them even more.

"You do agree, don't you, my darling?"

It took me a moment to realize Dominico had directed those words to me, and now I was expected to answer. I fumbled and stuttered for a few seconds, not knowing what to say.

"My dear, are you all right?" He still sounded gentle and caring.

I found I couldn't even answer that question, simple as it was. I could only stare at him. I was vaguely aware of Lorenzia's expression growing more and more angry.

"Of course you're not all right," Dominico said, placing his hand over mine in a loving gesture. "Your condition leaves you ill most of the time, I know, but please, I asked if you don't agree that the wedding should take place before your girth becomes too obvious?"

Why was he pretending to be so caring? I wondered. Then I saw Lorenzia's anger erupt, and I realized that his entire performance must have been aimed at her.

"She's with child?" Lorenzia banged her wine goblet so hard on the table it spilled over and made a livid circle the color of a cardinal's robe. She stood up and shouted at Dominico, "I warned you to stay out of that wench's bed, didn't I? And now you've shamed us. Making her pregnant before the wedding just as a common peasant would do. It serves you right to be shamed. You and that harridan both, but I deserve better."

A worm of a smile wiggled his mouth. "You deserve what I decide you deserve, my dear aunt, and where are your manners?" His tone was still smooth as congealed grease. "You should be congratulating the two of us on our good fortune. Perhaps you don't remember how happy you were when . . . Oh, forgive me; you were never blessed with this particular fortune, were you?"

Lorenzia's face grew pale, and I knew that he had pierced her with a poisoned weapon. She was obviously barren, and what woman wanted to be reminded of that? I have asked God's forgiveness a hundred times because of the pleasure I took in seeing her anger and chagrin. It seemed a recompense for her appearing so pleased by the bruises on my face. May

God forgive me again, for even now it gives me pleasure to re-member.

I saw very little of Dominico for the next two weeks be-cause of the wedding preparations. I was fitted for a new dress, which was to be made of heavy silk velvet dyed crimson. I was shocked when I heard that, because I knew from my experience in the market that crimson silk cost as much as two hundred head of swine.

A seamstress was called in to make the dress, as well as a new tunic, blue and woven with gold threads, for Dominico, and there were all kinds of preparations and plans going on for a banquet. I was no longer confined to my room, but I still felt far from free. While all the preparations were going on around me, there was nothing I could do except stand still for an occasional fitting and wander aimlessly around the house.

I took to spending time in the kitchen, where, although I wasn't supposed to, I helped occasionally by peeling turnips and slicing and trimming the meat. I became friends with Ru-fina, the cook, and even with Grimani, who sometimes came in to help. Grimani worked out a system to warn me when Do-minico drew close to the kitchen. He almost always worked near the arched doorway that was the entrance to the kitchen because the long butchering table was there. Butchering was his duty, since it required strength. When Dominico ap-proached, Grimani would strike a large iron cooking pot with his butchering knife, and I would hide in the larder or in one of the tall barrels that usually held wheat for grinding.

My time in the kitchen was the happiest I spent in those early months, and I often found myself wishing I'd discovered it sooner. Rufina was surprised at my abilities, and because of that I know it didn't take her long to confirm the gossip she'd heard that I was of lowly peasant stock. She never mentioned it, though. She was far too busy with other gossip. The more tragic or shocking or frightening the story she had to tell, the better she liked it.

I learned of someone named Alfonso who had been bitten by a snake and died a horrible, convulsive death. There was the wife of the silk merchant, who had a secret lover she met three times a week, and the son of a notary, recently jailed for sodomy. The last few days, however, there had been very little to gossip about, so she resorted to talking about the outbreak of the Black Death in a past year.

"The father of the wife of my husband's brother says it came up from the sea to the wharves in Porto Recanati and spread like locusto to the countryside. God's punishment for sinful ways, I say. And I say it's best to stay inside so it won't spread to you from strangers, for it's a terrible death. Sores in the groin and in the neck, and fever from the very pits of hell. The skin turning first red and then black. Old man Death plants and reaps in the same day. Why, a person can break his fast with his relatives in the morning, and by night he sups with his ancestors in heaven.

It's a punishment, I say to you, for God is not pleased with the sins of the world. It's a punishment."

I'd heard talk of the Black Death before, and the tales were always equally as frightening as Rufina's. My mother often told me of how her own mother died, coughing blood and covered with sores, her skin turning blacker and blacker as she neared death. Mama cried when she told that story, because, she said, she had refused to go near her mother. She slept outside, not even going in to eat, but took her meals from the river and from the fields until her mother and father both died and the house was burned. She would have starved to death, perhaps, or would have been eaten by a wild animal had my father not found her, wandering, half-crazed from hunger. He took her to his family's cottage and eventually married her.

My mother's health was never good, though. The long days of wandering the country hungry and alone took their toll. I had never in my life known her to be well or strong.

No one I knew was untouched by the Black Death, and we all feared it.

As my wedding date drew nearer, I had less time to spend in the kitchen with Rufina and less time to think about my fears. The fittings for my dress became more and more frequent. I grew tired of standing still for what seemed like hours every day while the seamstress fitted the bodice to my chest and the sleeves to the bodice and adjusted the skirt to accommodate my slightly larger waist. I also had to spend more time with Lorenzia while she coached me more on how to walk, how to talk, how to sit, when to smile, when not to smile. All of that made me unusually cross, and I snapped at Lorenzia more than once. Even I was surprised at that, but the changes going on in my body seemed to be affecting my mind and spirit.

I was also surprised at Lorenzia's reaction. I could tell she wanted to lash out at me with her words as well as her hand, but she held back. Dominico's attentiveness had made her afraid of me.

At night, all I could do was cry. My beautiful wedding gown made me think of Mama and Teresa and the new gowns they would never have and the wedding they would never see, all because Dominico was ashamed of them. I kept remembering little things that had happened, such as the way I had jerked away from Mama when she tried to touch me on that last day. If only I could have her near me now I would never move away from her touch again.

By the time my wedding day arrived, I was so exhausted I had to make an extra effort just to drag myself through the day. It started early, with a walk to the church. Dominico walked in front, dressed in his new clothes of blue and gold, and I walked behind him with Lorenzia next to me. Behind us followed all of Dominico's wealthy merchant friends dressed in their own finery.

We stopped in front of the church, and while we knelt on

the steps, two men I supposed to be Dominico's acquaintances unfurled an enormous swath of green damask and held it over our heads. In a little while the bishop in his white-and-gold robe emerged from the church and stood with us under the billowing green cloud.

I remember little of what he said and understood less, since he spoke in Latin, and I, a peasant, knew not the intricacies of that tongue. The rings we exchanged were made of gold, not copper, which was the metal used in the rings of peasant couples, including my own parents. Dominico had purchased both of the gold rings. The bishop wrapped his stole around them and blessed them and led us inside for the celebratory Mass.

As soon as I stepped into the dark, high-ceilinged cavern of the church, a feeling of dread grabbed me and squeezed my chest until I could hardly breathe. I felt a sudden urge to flee the church and run away, and I might have done so, embarrassing myself as well as Dominico, had I not noticed a young priest emerging from one of the small chapels along the side of the church. He saw me as well and gave me a gentle smile and a nod as a greeting. That small, almost inconsequential act of kindness calmed me. I tried to follow him with my eyes without turning my head, but he slipped away and must have left the church, for I never saw him again that day.

After the Mass, all the guests followed us back to Dominico's house and into his bedchamber, where the bishop blessed the bed with prayers and holy water. It was the first time I'd been inside Dominico's bedchamber. The walls were hung with tapestries just as the walls in the entrance hall of his house were, and there were several chests made of the finest wood situated around the room. The mattress on the wide bed was plump from the fresh straw that had been stuffed into it, and a coverlet of soft wool was laid atop it.

The rest is little more than a blur to me. Back in the grand *sala* there were wine and food and bawdy jokes, and then, while it was still midday, several women encircled me like wolves circling their prey and led me back to the bedroom.

"Don't look so frightened; you're no stranger to this room," one of them said. I recognized her as one of the women I'd met at the engagement party. Her remark made the other women laugh as they undressed me and unwound my hair.

"I heard she was a peasant he found in the fields," I heard another say. "I've heard her kind can't get enough. They even turn to the likes of sheep and young bulls."

"Oh, Clarise, you gossip so! Of course she's not a peasant. Look at her."

There was another laugh. "There'll be no need for young bulls now that she has one that stands on two feet," said the woman who put a soft white nightdress over my head and shoulders.

"And so handsome a bull at that," someone else said. "I'll bet he's handsome everywhere." She tugged at my arm. "Oh, do tell us what it looks like. Is it enormous?"

"Look, she's blushing," one of them said. "No need for that," she said, turning to me. "We all know what you've been doing. It's all over town that you're already carrying his child." Her voice was cruel.

"You must tell us what his shaft looks like! In a few months you'll lose your taste for it and forget that it was once handsome to you." This remark brought more bawdy laughter, and they might have gone on teasing me had there not been a loud knock at the door. Their laughter turned to twittering while they hurried to get me into the plump bed with my hair spread across the pillows they'd placed behind me.

"She's ready!" one of them called.

Dominico, smelling of wine, staggered into the room, and they all fluttered away in the swish, swish of silks. When they were gone Dominico ripped the coverlet back and looked down at me while he carelessly removed his own clothes. His swollen member pointed at me like an accusing finger, and then suddenly he was on top of me.

I pushed him off when I realized the wine had numbed his mind to the point that he had fallen asleep.

Chapter 7

M<small>Y LIFE</small>, for a while, became easier. As the weeks grew into months and my girth expanded with the child growing inside me, Dominico's anger cooled, and I was not subjected to his cruel blows. He took great pleasure in being seen with me and would even pat my expanding belly with what might have been mistaken for affection when we were in public. At home he mostly left me alone, except occasionally to call for me to dine with him and Lorenzia.

As for Lorenzia, she also avoided me for the most part. I spent more and more time in the kitchen with Rufina or in the garden, where Fausta would sometimes join me, occasionally even at Dominico's request, because he felt my condition made me weak and vulnerable. In truth, I didn't feel either weak or vulnerable. The morning sickness of the early weeks had passed, and I felt quite well, although I still had oddly changeable moods. Rufina told me my feeling of well-being was because I was in the time of quickening.

"Be grateful for these few weeks; they're gone soon enough," she said. "You're in the easy time now. The morning sickness has passed and your belly's not yet heavy enough to

99

make you miserable. It's God's gift to a woman with child—a few weeks peace to feel the baby quicken."

She was right. The quickening came early one morning just as I stood up from my bed. I felt a fluttering inside my womb, soft as the wing of a butterfly, and I understood that I had just witnessed a miracle. A life had been created inside me, and now it was moving. I stood still and quiet for several minutes, waiting for it to happen again, and when it did I saw, for the briefest of moments, the Virgin smiling at me. She appeared amidst a streak of morning light shining in my open window. I was overwhelmed with joy for that appearance and that smile, as well as for the confirmation of life moving inside me, so overwhelmed, in fact, that for a moment I thought I would burst with happiness.

I told no one at first about either of the miracles—the movement of life inside me or the smile of the Virgin, but I had an intense desire to kneel before her image in the church and offer my thanks. We attended Mass almost every week, but I had never been to the church alone. Dominico always wanted an eye on me when I went out. On a few occasions he'd allowed me out under the supervision of the signora. The pretense for all of that watchfulness was that it was for my protection. I thought it was a kind of insurance against my embarrassing him by doing or saying something only a peasant would do or say.

I asked for permission to go to church, but, just as I expected, Dominico refused to allow it unless Lorenzia went with me.

"But she doesn't like to go with me," I protested.

"She'll do as I say." He was busy with his accounts and spoke without looking up from them. "Lorenzia!" he bellowed, still not looking up. She appeared quickly. "She wants to go to church. You are to go with her," he said, glancing up for the first time.

I saw Lorenzia start to protest, but she pressed her lips together and gave me an icy stare.

"Go! Go!" Dominico said, waving us out. His attention had already turned back to his work.

I was waiting at the front door in my cap and shawl when Lorenzia appeared, wearing a hooded cloak and an angry scowl. I was no happier to have her along than she was to accompany me. We stepped outside into the wind that had grown its autumn teeth and made our way to the church, following the route we took each Sunday with the rest of the household. Dominico insisted that we all attend Mass. It wouldn't do, he said, for word to get around that he was not a pious man.

"Mateo, that wool merchant who came here from Florence, saw his business drop by half when it became known that he was lax in his attendance of Mass." He spoke those words like a warning to himself, and he saw to it that the spectacle of his entire household walking to church and attending services was exhibited each Sunday. I was part of the show. This time I wanted no exhibition. I simply wanted to pray.

The church, smelling faintly of incense, was quiet and dark except for a few candles flickering at the front. While Lorenzia waited and sulked, I made my way to the little chapel of the Virgin at the side of the church and knelt at her feet. I still had no gift for prayer and was never certain I did it right. I simply let myself feel the joy I'd felt earlier, for seeing the brief vision and for feeling the quickening, and somehow I felt she knew my gratitude even if I could not express it in pretty words.

I'm not sure how long I stayed there, but when I crossed myself and stood up to leave, I felt a lightness of my spirit that I hadn't felt in a long time. It was not until I walked out of the chapel and into the main sanctuary that I saw the young priest again. He was kneeling before a statue of the suffering Christ near the front of the church. I hadn't seen him since the first time he smiled at me on the day of my wedding, but I recognized his profile and remembered how that smile, that small act of kindness, had helped me get through what was otherwise a dreadful day. Seeing him again surprised me. I had assumed he was one of the mendicants who passed through town from time to time, usually on their way to the monastery in the mountains just outside San Severino. I was puzzled as to why he was not there now.

I had to awaken Lorenzia, who'd fallen asleep at the back, and by the time we reached Dominico's house—I still had trouble thinking of it as my home—I had forgotten about the priest. I was basking in the double joy of the vision and the quickening. I felt as if the light of heaven shone all around me. Rufina must have noticed it, too.

"Now look at you!" Her voice was a tinkling bell. "You're all aglow. If I didn't know better, I'd say you've been out to meet a lover."

It was shocking that she would say such a thing to me, and, as the mistress of the house, I most certainly should have scolded her at the least, and most likely should have told my husband and had her thrown out. But I knew she meant no harm—knew, too, that it was my fault for allowing her to become so familiar and friendly with me. Besides, I was feeling far too full of happiness to scold anyone. I could only laugh at her remark.

"No lover could make me this happy," I said. "I've been talking to the Holy Mother. I've been to church."

Rufina gave me a long, scrutinizing look. "That smile on your face. It says it all. You felt the babe move." Now she was smiling, too.

"Yes!" I said with another little laugh I couldn't contain. "A few days ago, and at almost the same time, I think I saw the Virgin. She was standing in the light of my—"

A sudden loud thumping followed by a chilling wail like

the sound of death came from somewhere above us, and then both sounds repeated again and again.

Rufina's face darkened. "God have mercy," she said, and crossed herself.

"What is it?" I asked, too frightened to do more than whisper.

Rufina only shook her head and bit her lip. Both of us, as well as Grimani, who was busy on the opposite side of the kitchen, waited in silence for several seconds. I still had no idea of what the awful sound could have been. Before I could ask again, Grimani's spoon stuttered a warning on the cooking pot. Rufina's eyes widened, and I headed for the larder.

Grimani's warning, of course, meant that Dominico was approaching the kitchen, and although I still didn't know what had caused the hellish sound, I knew without understanding why that he was somehow connected to it. I could hear the blood rushing in my head and my heart pounding a wild fury as I hid in the darkness of the little room. Yet somehow, above those sounds, I could also hear footsteps on the stone floor as someone entered the kitchen. There were muffled voices and someone crying. None of the voices sounded like Dominico's, and I was almost certain it was Fausta who was crying. I didn't dare open the door to look out, and when I heard footsteps approaching the larder, I tried to hide behind a shank of beef hanging from the ceiling.

I almost fainted with relief when the door opened and I

saw Rufina standing there. Her expression was grim, but she motioned with her head that I was to come out of the larder. "You'd best go now," she whispered.

Just as I stepped out into the kitchen, I heard crying again, and knew without a doubt that it was Fausta. I saw her slumped to the floor with Grimani kneeling beside her, trying to comfort her.

I ran toward her. "Fausta, what's . . . ?" I stopped when I saw her swollen face and the blood streaming from her nose. A gash under her eye was also oozing blood. I knew without asking what had happened. "He did this," I said.

Fausta nodded.

"Why?" I knelt beside her along with Grimani and tried to wipe her face with my hand.

"Said I stole from him." Her mouth was so swollen it was difficult for her to talk.

"Stole what?"

"Food." It was Rufina who answered, as if she wanted to spare Fausta the pain of speaking. At the same time she handed me a damp cloth.

"It wasn't much," Fausta said as I bathed her face. "Only a loaf of bread."

"Foolish child! I told you you'd get caught, didn't I?" Rufina was crying as she spoke, and she pulled the cloth from my hand and took over the task of wiping Fausta's face herself.

"Why would you steal a loaf of bread?" I asked, trying to

get out of Rufina's way. "There's always plenty for you to eat here. Even Dominico doesn't deny you your rations."

Fausta shook her head. "Wasn't for me. Was for them."

"For them?" I was puzzled.

"Them what's outside."

Still, I could make no sense of what she was saying, but before I could ask more, Rufina stood and pulled me up with her.

"She's talking about her kin," Rufina whispered. "You'd best go, like I said, my lady. Don't let him catch you down here."

"But . . ."

"Go, please. You'll only make it worse if he sees you here."

There was such urgency in her voice I dared not protest. Also, I knew she was right. If Dominico found me there, he could and would punish us all, if for no other reason than that I was trying to comfort Fausta.

I didn't see Fausta for the rest of the day. Dominico didn't go back to his office on the ground floor below the house where he usually spent most of his day. Instead he stayed in one of the rooms upstairs where he often received guests. The guests he received today were all men who carried leather-bound ledgers and talked about the cost of things. Lorenzia didn't go out either, as she often did, but confined herself to her room.

Because of the close presence of both of them, I was unable to go down to the kitchen again, and I was left to ponder why Fausta had stolen the bread for someone "outside." Someone Rufina said was her kin. When Dominico, Lorenzia, and I gathered for our supper in the early evening, Lorenzia brought up the matter.

"You finally caught that wench stealing from your kitchen. I told you weeks ago what she was doing, remember?"

"Mmmmff," Dominico said, stuffing bread sopped in broth into his mouth.

"If you had listened to me then, you'd have saved yourself enough bread to feed us for a month."

Dominico ignored her. He dipped more bread in the broth, this time skimming off the thin layer of grease that had formed at the top.

"What do you think she was doing with it, anyway?" Lorenzia asked.

"Eating it, I suppose." Dominico sounded oddly disinterested in spite of all the energy he'd put into beating poor Fausta.

"No, she wasn't," Lorenzia said. "She was giving it to those miserable paupers near the market square and outside the market gate."

Dominico inspected his grease-coated morsel of bread. "If you knew that, why did you ask?" he said as he popped the bread into his mouth.

So that was what Fausta had meant when she said "them what's outside." I remembered the people outside the walls of the city whom I'd seen the day Dominico first brought me there. The ones Dominico's driver had forced away from the cart with his whip. The ones Dominico had called vermin. I re-membered how poor they looked and how hungry—even poorer and hungrier than I had ever been. Those people were Fausta's kin?

I felt embarrassed and ashamed that I had forgotten about those poor souls until now, and even more distraught to think how Fausta had not forgotten and had risked so much to help them.

"I certainly hope the beating wasn't too late," I heard Lorenzia say when I turned my attention back to the conversa-tion at the table. "I hope she doesn't think she can get away with it again."

"Oh, she certainly won't do it again. At least not in my house," Dominico said. "I've thrown her out. She's on the streets by now looking for something to feed herself."

I was so upset I could no longer eat my own bread and broth. I couldn't even look at Lorenzia to see what I imagined would be cruel satisfaction on her face.

"No more talk of unpleasant things," Dominico said, glancing at me with a possessive smile. "We mustn't say things to upset Margherita; it could mark the child."

He was right, of course. Everyone knew that if a pregnant woman was frightened or made distraught about something, the child would be marked by it. That could mean my child would grow up to be a thief like Fausta, or it could mean eat-ing bread would make him sick or that he would have too great a fondness for bread. It could cause any of a number of things I could not and should not think about. For that reason I should put the incident out of my mind.

I found that impossible. Later, after everyone was in bed and the house was dark, I made my way down to the servants' quarters next to the kitchen. I wanted to see Fausta again before she left, but I was too late.

Rufina awakened and sat up from her pallet as I approached the room where she and Fausta slept. "She's gone," she whispered.

"Where? Where has she gone?" I was desperate with worry about her.

"To the streets, maybe. Or outside the gates where she can lie in the dirt with the rest of her kin. Or maybe to the river to drown herself. How should I know?" Rufina's voice had gone bitter with anger and worry.

"I must find her," I said.

"Don't be a fool. Go back to bed." Rufina lay down on her pallet and pulled a blanket over her head. I made my way upstairs again, trying to decide how I would go about finding her. I couldn't bear the thought of her being alone, hungry, and frightened, with nowhere to turn.

I knew I had to look for her, but how would I get out of the house? Other merchants' wives went out alone to attend church or to go to the market or to visit friends. No one kept as close a watch on a wife as Dominico. Besides worrying that

I would embarrass him, I think he was also afraid I would run away if I were ever let out on my own. In truth, I cannot say his fear was unreasonable. I would have welcomed any opportunity to find my way home. I wanted to be with Mama when my baby was born. There were hundreds of questions I wanted to ask her. Rufina had been my substitute mother and attempted to answer everything I asked, but it was not the same as confiding in my own mother. I no longer dreamed of marrying Augustino, and I could not say why, except that in the few short months I'd been away I seemed to have grown beyond him.

I slept very little that night because I was so worried about Fausta. In spite of my wakefulness, no clear and ingenious plan of how to find her came to me. The first weak light of morning had just made a timid appearance when I got out of bed. Though I had at first been embarrassed by having her help me dress, now that I knew she wouldn't be coming to help me I felt helpless with grief. I walked to the window and stared down at the garden, as I often did when I was troubled. It was still my favorite spot, and until the days had grown too cool, I spent long hours there with the birds and with my reluctant saints. It was no longer necessary for me to climb out my window and down the vine to enjoy the garden, since Dominico at least allowed me to venture that far.

I had never found a way to escape the garden, though. That, of course, was why Dominico trusted me to go there.

Nevertheless, it was vast enough that I felt less imprisoned than I did in the house. That reason compelled me to go to the garden at that moment.

I dressed quickly in the new dress Dominico had arranged to be made for me. It was sewn of the finest wool, soft and luxurious with a cut that hung loosely from beneath my breasts in order to accommodate my expanding womb. Next I pulled on the leather shoes, my most prized possession. They were beautiful, and protected my feet in a way my rough peasant's shoes had never done. Last, I slipped into a warm overdress made of heavier wool to protect me from the November chill.

I was dressing for more than just a few moments of meditation alone in the garden. I was being driven there by the blind faith that I would somehow find a way out. And if I found my way out I could find Fausta, I reasoned, although I knew even then that my thinking was unsound. Still, before I left the house, I went by the kitchen and took a loaf of the previous day's bread, which, although it was already a little stale, was still edible.

I didn't find an exit immediately. At first I sat on the ornate little bench under the chestnut tree, my usual place. I was restless and too cold to stay under the naked, leafless tree, so I stood and walked with brisk steps around the garden. I found myself looking, as I'd often done, for a secret gate or a door hidden among the vines that crawled along the walls. As before, I found nothing. The only way to enter or exit the garden was from the ground floor of the house.

Or so I thought.

My foot caught in the tangled web of a leafless vine as I made my way around the garden, and before I knew it I fell, pitching forward until I was on my knees, dropping the bread and pushing my hands into dirt and gravel to break my fall. I managed to emit only a little cry, not enough to wake the house, but I was much chagrined at the way my palms stung and were even bleeding a little. I'd gone soft in the few months I'd been Dominico's prisoner wife. When my hands were toughened by work in the fields, such a minor little tumble would have been nothing to me, and it certainly wouldn't have brought blood. It wasn't just the gravel that had made my hands bleed, I realized, when I saw several pieces of sharp-edged slate lying around.

The pieces were partially covered with dirt and tufts of grass and the matted and twisted little branches of the vine. They must have been scraps carelessly discarded by workmen when they built the slate roof for the house. The more I looked at them, the less they looked like roofing slate and the more they looked like stepping-stones. Within seconds I was back on my feet, scurrying to find as many pieces as I could and stacking them against the wall until I had a surface I could stand on. Once on top of the stack, with just a little effort I could reach the top of the wall with my hands. I tossed the loaf to the other side, but it took considerable strength to pull myself up with my arms until I could get a knee and then a foot on top of the wall.

I tore my dress and scraped my knee as I scrambled over and then jumped down into the alley behind the fence. When I retrieved the bread and straightened, I was surprised to feel a catch in my back, probably from lifting and stacking the pieces of slate—another signal I'd become soft, or else a consequence of my growing belly. There was no one around to see me, only a donkey who had obviously strayed from his pen. He was nibbling at tufts of grass that grew in the spaces between the stones of the wall. I hurried along the alley headed for the street. The donkey followed me a short distance until he was distracted by a basket of vegetables behind a little wooden fence that separated the back of one of the houses from the alley. Finally I saw a street stretching in front of me.

I recognized the street. It was one I'd walked along with Dominico. I remembered that a short distance down another street intersected, and I thought that by turning left I would eventually reach the market square. I had not been allowed to visit the market since I'd become Dominico's property, although I had asked permission to go with Rufina more than once. He must have suspected that my motive was to find my family, because he always forbade it. Yet I still remembered the route we took when I first came to his house.

As soon as I reached the intersection I turned down Market

Street, not because I thought anyone would be there at such an early hour, but because a short distance beyond the square there was a gate in the city wall—the same place where I'd seen all the poor beggars when I first arrived. Maybe they were the same people on the "outside" whom Fausta had mentioned. Maybe she was among them now.

It took much longer than I expected to reach the market square, and before I came to the wall I could see that the gate was closed. I should have expected it, of course. After all, what good are a wall and a gate to a town if they aren't closed and secure? I was angry at myself and disappointed. All I could do was cry. Foolish, I know, but, as I have mentioned, there was something about having a child in my belly that affected my moods and kept the tears pushed just to the brim of my eyes.

I was sitting on the ground sobbing when I noticed, through the blur of my tears, something in the distance, in the square. When I dried my eyes with the backs of my hands, I could see that it was not one, but two people walking along gathering up something from the ground. As I stood and walked toward them, I realized that there were more than two. There were at least half a dozen, and I knew what they were doing: They were foraging for something to eat. I should have remembered how clever and resourceful one is when one is hungry. Obviously the poor lived among us both inside and outside the walls.

I pulled up my skirt and ran toward them, shouting, "You! You, there! I'm looking for someone. A woman called . . ."

As soon as they heard and then saw me, they all scurried away, disappearing as if they'd never been there at all.

"I have bread. See? I have bread." I waved the now dirty loaf above my head, but no one reappeared. I walked around the square, stopping at a deserted booth here and there, finding no one. Eventually I sat down and leaned against one of the trees that lined the square and waited for what seemed like a very long time. I saw a figure once—someone who looked surprisingly like the young priest I'd seen twice before—but he disappeared into the shadows. When, after a long wait, I saw no one else, I left the bread on a counter of one of the booths and walked away.

Once I reached Dominico's house, it didn't take me long to realize that scaling the garden wall from the outside would be impossible. There were no odd pieces of slate lying around for me to use as stepping-stones. The only thing I could think to do was pray, and since I was afraid the Holy Mother would think of me as a disobedient sinner, it would have to be Saint Mary of Magdala I sought.

"You must help me," I whispered. "I know I was wrong to disobey Dominico. I know disobedience is a sin, and I cannot promise not to do it again, but you were a sinner once, and you know how easy it is for a girl to get herself into things. Maybe you will help. Just this once. Please."

Nothing happened.

I thought of praying again, but there seemed nothing more to say. I was going to have to get inside soon, though, because, while there was still only the donkey nibbling at the grass in the chinks of the wall, in a short while merchants and shoppers would be out on the streets. I couldn't risk anyone who knew Dominico seeing me.

The front courtyard gate would be locked, and even if it wasn't, I couldn't just walk in the front door. There was the back door, of course, the one that opened into the alley, and the one the servants used, but it would be locked at this hour, too, because now that the weather had cooled Rufina made a habit of keeping it closed all day.

My heart pounded with anxiety as I paced back and forth along the wall, and to make matters worse the donkey began to annoy me by nudging at me. I suppose he was looking for something more to eat than the few tufts of grass and weeds he'd found in the wall. I had swatted his nose and tried to push him away a number of times before I realized that here was my salvation.

If I could get the beast to stand still against the wall for even a short time, I could stand on his back and boost myself up. That should be easy enough. By reaching my arm through the line of posts, I was able to steal a few vegetables from the basket behind the wooden gate across the street. I placed the vegetables against the wall, and while the donkey nibbled at them, I climbed up and stood on his back and boosted myself over the wall, feeling grateful that I was still agile enough, in spite of my condition, to do that. I jumped into the garden, landing on my hands and knees. My head was still down when I realized that directly in front of me were two legs and a pair of black boots.

Chapter 8

"BEHOLD! A woman has fallen from above and is now kneeling at my feet," the man said.

"Oh, it's you, Grimani, thank God." I stood and tried to brush the dust from my skirt.

"And what would you have done had it not been me, but the master instead?" Grimani's knotted fists were on his hips in an angry manner, and his face looked equally knotted with anger.

"I . . . well, I—"

Grimani interrupted my stammering response. "You would have suffered another beating, you would. Sometimes I think the devil has possessed you to make you indulge in such wild actions. Jump off a fence, will you? And you with child. It's a good thing you're of sturdy peasant stock if you're going to act like a young boy with such antics. Most merchants' wives are so soft they must keep themselves confined and don't lift a finger when they've a babe in their belly." He shook his head in a mixture of relief and anger.

"I'm truly sorry, Grimani. I didn't mean to worry you. And you needn't think I will hurt myself," I added. "A woman with child is not as fragile as you think. Why, I've seen plenty of them work hard as a man in the fields all day and birth a healthy child that night."

"Peasants, they are. As I said, it's a good thing you're of the same stock." He grabbed my arm and pulled me toward the house. "Now get inside before the master sees you, and give thanks to God and all the saints he hasn't seen you already. I've been meaning to clear out that old batch of slate for months, and the minute I saw 'em stacked there I knew what you'd done." He shook his head in disbelief and led me with his firm hand into the house through the back door.

Rufina met us with a worried frown. "Where was she?"

"It's best you don't ask," Grimani said, then proceeded to tell her. "Jumped the wall, she did, then jumped back in again."

"What? No mortal could—"

Grimani laughed. "Oh, she's mortal, all right. Made herself stepping-stones out of the scraps of slate in the garden."

"I told you long ago to clean that up," Rufina said, venting her anger at him before she turned to me. "And you." She shook her head. "You've no business climbing around in your condition. And look at your dress!" She gave a quick glance over her shoulder. "What were you thinking? If the master finds out . . . What cause did you have to go over the wall?"

"I . . . I only wanted to go to church," I said, deciding not to worry her more by telling her I was looking for Fausta. "I wanted to pray at the foot of the Virgin. I wanted to give thanks for the quickening."

"Church, you say?" Her voice was less agitated. My lie had calmed her.

"Church," I said. "To pray."

Rufina shook her head, and I could see worry forming behind her eyes. "Church or not, you're asking for trouble if the master finds out. He'll beat you again, and Grimani and me as well. He'll say we're to blame for letting you out."

"Oh, no," I said, alarmed. "I could never allow that to happen."

Rufina glanced over her shoulder again. "If you don't mind me telling you, child, er, I mean, my lady, it's best you ask the signora to accompany you if you want to go to church."

I could only stare at her without responding. The thought of having an impatient Lorenzia watching over me again while I prayed was distasteful to me, and I certainly couldn't ask her to go searching for Fausta with me. But if I was putting Rufina and Grimani in danger, then I had to be more thoughtful.

By evening I had convinced myself that I could ask Dominico again for permission to go to the church alone. I had also convinced myself that even Dominico could not deny such a pure and pious request forever. If I couldn't convince myself that it wasn't a sin to deceive him by taking that opportunity to scour the streets for Fausta, then I just wouldn't think about it.

"You want to go to church again?" he said that night as we took our supper. "Isn't Sunday Mass enough for you?"

"I wish to learn more piety—for the sake of my . . . of our child." The little lie was as much for Lorenzia's benefit as Dominico's.

Dominico grumbled something incomprehensible, then said nothing at all to me for the rest of the evening. It was several days later before I found the opportunity to ask him again, since I did not always dine with him and, in fact, didn't even see him on some days when he worked late. He had, for a while, insisted that we share his bed, but of late he'd taken to allowing me to sleep in my own room. He made a show of letting everyone in the house know that it was out of consideration for me and my condition, while I secretly suspected that it was meant to spare himself more humiliation. Of course, being relatively free of him as I was, it occurred to me to go without his permission, but after what Grimani had said, I was afraid to jeopardize him and Rufina.

Finally, one night I happened upon an opportunity to speak to Dominico. It was well past supper, when the rest of the house had gone to bed, including the servant who had taken Fausta's place, an unpleasant woman called Concetta, who constantly groveled before Dominico and Lorenzia. I, feeling restless and unable to sleep, was pacing the house in my nightgown, wrapped in a shawl against the cold. I walked by the open doorway to the office and saw him at his desk. The room, lit only by a single candle, was a gloomy cave where even the fire had gone out, and Dominico sat slumped at his desk. At first I thought he was asleep, and I tried to hurry past the door before he awoke. He saw me before I could get away.

"Margherita!" His voice was slurred, and he motioned with an unsteady hand for me to step inside.

I did, reluctantly, and soon saw the empty wine bottle on his desk as well as the overturned glass, spilling out the last drops of the purple liquid on one of his documents.

"What keeps you up so late?" he asked in his drunken voice.

Grimani and Rufina's warning to me about how they would be beaten for my misbehaving had rendered me even more afraid of him, so that I could barely stammer out a few incomprehensible words.

"I . . . I was just . . . uh, that is . . ."

"You've grown damnably restless lately." He leaned forward, his eyes fixed on me. "What is it you want?"

I took a breath, trying to conjure the answer he wanted— the answer that would keep him from doing something vile. Before I could think of what to say he spoke again.

"Wanting to go to the church to pray, are you? Go! Go to church, damn you. Go as much as you like." He waved his arm in an unsteady gesture. "Whore that you are, you'd best pray as much as you can. Now get out of my sight."

I hurried away from him, but before I could leave the room he called to me.

"Margherita, wait!"

I turned around slowly. I was surprised that his angry expression had turned to sadness.

"Margherita, I . . ." His voice was contrite, and I thought for a moment that he was about to apologize for speaking to me with such rudeness, but he seemed unable to go on. Instead he dropped his head into his hands. He was having one of his headaches, I thought. The wine, no doubt, was making it worse, but I dared not remind him of that. Without looking up and without saying anything more, he signaled me with a wave to leave.

I left immediately without saying a word, and the next morning I was up early and dressed in my warmest clothes. I left through the front door before anyone, save the servants, was out of bed. I was carrying my loaf of bread concealed in my cloak. Concetta was the only one who saw me, and she gave me a look that was half scowl and half question as I left.

My plan, flimsy as it might be, was to go back to the market square to try to find someone who knew Fausta and where I could find her. I worried about her almost constantly, especially now that winter was coming. The cold would make her cough worse, I thought. Did she have shelter or warm clothes? Did she have enough food to eat? Had she been able to find another position? The latter, I knew, was unlikely, since she would have no references, and Dominico undoubtedly would have told everyone he knew that she was not fit for employment.

First, though, I would go to the church, just as I had led Dominico to believe. I looked forward to the Virgin looking down on me with what I imagined to be tenderness as I prayed.

The church was cold and dark, except for a few candles burning at the front near the altar, but I wrapped my cloak tighter around me and walked to the little chapel and knelt at the Virgin's feet. I prayed for several minutes before I began to feel that there was someone watching me. I even glanced over my shoulder twice, but I saw no one. Finally I felt so uncomfortable and so convinced that someone else was in the church that I stood and made my way to the door, eager to leave.

I walked a short distance beyond the church when I glanced back again. This time I saw someone. It was the young priest. He must have been the one I sensed behind me in the church. His arms were folded in front of him and obscured by his sleeves. The wind had blown his cowl back, and he walked now with his head down as if to shield himself from the cold wind while he moved toward me with a steady purpose. I waited for him, thinking he would approach me, but he turned down a side street without looking up.

With a shrug, I continued on my way to the market square. When I arrived it appeared empty, but I soon saw a few souls huddled together near one of the stalls. As I got closer I could see that they were warming themselves around a small fire that was struggling for life against the awakening wind. I walked a little closer, then called out, thinking it best not to make them think I was trying to sneak up on them.

"Hello!" I waved my loaf of bread.

Heads turned toward me, and immediately some of the group disappeared. The few who were left continued to watch me closely as I drew nearer.

"You must be hungry. And cold," I said, holding the bread out to them. "I've brought—"

"Hungry? And cold?" The tall, gaunt woman who had spoken those words laughed. "Now, what ever made you think that?" A little girl with curly hair and deep-set eyes stood next to her. She was about the same age as my sister, Teresa, and the curly hair reminded me of her.

The others laughed at the woman's sarcasm. It was not a merry sound, but bitter, infused with the same ice that was in the wind that buffeted us. All of their eyes were trained on the bread I held.

"Here," I said, thrusting it toward one of them. "I was hoping you could tell me if you knew of—"

The words were scarcely out of my mouth before the little girl rushed forward, grabbed the bread from my hand, and ran. I could see her tearing off big chunks of it with her teeth as she disappeared among the stalls that lined the square. In almost the same moment the others ran after her.

I'd seen that kind of hunger before. It could turn people into animals. I'd even felt the temptation to hoard food for myself in the past when the crops were poor and my stomach was empty. I could never bear to see the look on the faces of the others in my family when they were hungry, though, especially Teresa, so if I ever came upon a morsel in hard times I shared it. Also, even in the most desperate circumstances, I'd been taught to show my gratitude to anyone who tried to help me. Not run away like an animal.

"They don't trust you."

"What?" I turned around quickly toward the voice that had spoken those words and saw the young priest. "Did you follow me here?" I asked, feeling uneasy. "I saw you leave the church and—"

"Yes," he said. "I followed you."

"Why?"

"I thought you might need some help."

"Well," I said, relaxing a little. "That was kind of you, but I doubt that you can help me. You see, I'm looking for someone, and I thought I might find her here. Or at least someone who knows her."

"I'm afraid you're not going to get anything from these people, Signora Vasari. As I said, they don't trust you."

"How did you know my name?"

"Your husband is a prominent man, signora. Everyone in San Severino knows who you are."

I didn't doubt what he said. After all, Dominico *was* quite well-known, but the idea of everyone knowing who I was made me feel uncomfortable.

"That . . . that may or may not be the case," I stammered, "but it still doesn't explain why you think I need help."

He smiled, and as he did so he stepped a little closer to me. It was then that I saw that his eyes were a jolting blue. I had never seen such eyes, although I'd heard of them. Mama told me people from the north had blue eyes because the cold had turned them to ice. I didn't think that was true, because it gets cold in San Severino and even snows sometimes, and I'd never seen anyone with blue eyes there. Besides, the priest's eyes didn't look like ice. They were more like blue fire.

"Didn't you just tell me you need help finding someone?" he asked.

I got the feeling he was laughing at me. He must have thought I was a child. Straightening my shoulders and trying to look as tall as possible, I said, "As a matter of fact, I did say that, but I don't see how you could have possibly known that when you followed me from the church."

"Is that what you were doing when you were here before? Looking for someone?"

"I *knew* I saw you here before," I said, pointing a finger at him.

"Indeed. And you looked as if you needed help then, too."

"You were spying on me?"

He smiled at me again, and a little laugh rolled up from his throat. "Not spying. I was here trying to help, and you happened along. It looked as if you were trying to help as well. But you were going about it wrong, just as you were a moment ago."

"What do you mean?"

"As I said, they don't trust you."

"But—"

"Look at you in all your finery, your warm cloak, your leather shoes. Most people who look like you do just want to kick them and get them out of the way."

"They took my bread." I sounded defensive.

"Yes. They're hungry. I doubt you can understand that."

"Of course I understand that," I said, still defensive.

"Not unless you've really been hungry, and I doubt you have."

I didn't respond at first. I was thinking how easily he judged me without knowing me, how surprising it was that he didn't see me for what I was—a peasant who understood hunger all too well.

"My dress, my shoes, that frightens them?"

"Yes," he said. "As I told you, they . . ."

He went on talking, but I wasn't listening. I was thinking he was right. I could remember how frightened and leery I had sometimes been of the rich and well dressed—how cruel they could be at times, treating us as if we were no more than cattle.

"I don't want to frighten anyone," I said, interrupting the priest.

He was silent for a moment as he studied my face. "No," he said at length, "I'm sure you don't."

"How do you know about these people?" I asked.

"I'm one of them," he said, "a mendicant monk. I've taken a vow of poverty."

I shook my head, studying him, his tall, muscular body, his sparkling eyes, his hands, strong but unblemished by hard work. "But you weren't born to it," I said.

His eyes widened in a brief show of surprise that I had guessed the truth. "No," he said, "I was not born to it. My father was a wealthy merchant, just as your husband is."

"Then why—"

"A merchant's life seemed empty to me. So much concentration on money and possessions. Life has more meaning than daily bread."

"I see," I said, although I did not see his point at all. I had spent most of my life trying to secure my daily bread.

"I hunger for truth. Knowledge. The beauty of brotherly love."

"Mmm."

"And there is, of course, the need to feed the hungry, clothe the naked, heal the sick."

"Oh, yes!" I said, understanding at last. "I want to do that, too. That's what got Fausta thrown out, you see. She was trying to feed the hungry, while I had given very little thought to them since I arrived, because, of course, I've been ill with . . . But what she did made me remember how others need my help, and now I have to find her as well, because since my husband . . . Well, what I mean is, I worry about her being cold and hungry and . . ." I was rattling on, so happy to have found someone who might understand how I felt. Unfortunately, judging from the look on the poor priest's face, I was not making very much sense at all.

"Fausta?" he said, still giving me his questioning look.

"My . . . servant," I said. The words felt strange on my tongue. I still could not think of myself as someone with servants.

"You say she was thrown out. Why?"

"Because she . . . she did something to displease my husband."

"Something sinful?"

"Oh, no! I mean, yes. Well, it depends upon what you call a sin."

The priest frowned. "A sin is a sin, madam."

"No. It's not always so simple."

"Explain."

"You see," I said, "she stole bread from the kitchen."

"Stealing is a sin."

"To feed the hungry."

"Ah, the devil enters now," the priest said.

"What?"

"He loves to confuse us by making sin appear not to be a sin."

131

I could see now, for the first time, that in spite of his frown his eyes were laughing.

"How can the devil, or anyone, make sin not a sin? Isn't that what you were trying to say to me a moment ago?"

This time the priest laughed out loud. "Ah, I can see that you have a keen mind. You can beat me at my own game."

"Game?"

"Forgive me, signora, I was toying with you. I'm afraid it's a bad habit I have—indulging in mental jousting. I must ask forgiveness." I got the feeling he didn't mean to ask me or God, either, for forgiveness. He was enjoying himself too much. "You're right, of course," he continued, "stealing bread to feed the hungry is not necessarily a sin. Remember how the Holy Bible teaches us that our Lord took grain from the fields when he was hungry?"

"I know little of the Bible, Father, except that it teaches us to love God and to love others as we love ourselves."

"Then you know the essence of all, Signora Vasari." He smiled at me with his mouth and his bright eyes.

"Please don't call me that."

He looked surprised. "Is that not your name?"

"My name is Margherita."

"Then I shall call you Margherita. And you must call me Father Colin."

It was a harsh-sounding foreign name that I didn't try to pronounce.

"I will try to help you find Fausta," he said. "If she is cold and hungry, then we must find her. Come with me," he said, reaching for my arm and leading me toward the place where the others had fled.

"Wait," I said, holding back. "There's something I must do first."

He gave me a surprised look while I removed my soft leather shoes and my warm woolen cloak and loosened my hair from its elaborate twist. I folded my cloak and shoes into a bundle and walked barefooted toward the group of people who were shivering and quarreling over the last bit of bread.

Chapter 9

At first all they could do was stare at me as if I were some kind of spectacle in my bare feet and with my unkempt hair. All those eyes leveled on me, all those unreadable expressions, made me uneasy.

"I didn't mean to frighten you," I said finally. I hardly recognized my own voice, it was so choked with the uncertainty I felt.

There was a long silence, and I kept wondering why Father Colin, who stood behind me, didn't say something. He was as mute as the rest of them.

"Don't scare me none," a voice said. It took me a moment to realize it was the same woman who had mocked me with her sarcasm earlier. She no longer sounded mocking, and she was looking at me with more of a questioning expression than the suspicious one I'd noticed before.

"You got more bread?" It was the little girl who reminded me of Teresa.

"No," I said, looking her in the eye, "but I can bring more tomorrow."

"What you want from us?" It was the tall man who asked, and he had not lost his expression of suspicion.

135

I was about to answer that I wanted help finding Fausta, but I felt Father Colin's hand in the small of my back. I took it as a signal not to speak.

"This woman wants nothing from you," the priest said in his accented Italian. "She is here because I brought her." That was the first time I'd ever heard a priest tell a lie. He hadn't really brought me here. I would have come without him. "Her name is Margherita. You see, she comes to you barefooted to show her humility and her desire to help."

There was another silence while the man, as well as the others, considered what the priest said. "Everybody wants something," the man said, looking at me with his still-suspicious eyes.

"She wants to help," Father Colin said, "and in particular she wants to help her friend called Fausta."

The woman with the little girl laughed. It was a hard, cruel sound. "You think you can help Fau—"

"We don't know nobody by that name," the man said, cutting her off. The woman ducked her head and backed away. At almost the same moment the little girl spoke.

"You're a crazy old man, Benno. Course we know Fausta. She's the one what had to go to—"

Before she could finish, the woman struck the child hard on her face. The little girl staggered backward, wiping a bit of blood from her lip, but refusing even to whimper.

"We don't know nobody by that name," the man said

again. This time his eyes were cold, and his mouth was a narrow, bloodless slit.

"We'll be going, then," Father Colin said. At the same time I felt his hand grip my arm and give me a firm tug. "God bless you all," he said, turning me around and forcing me to walk away from the group. He gave another pull on my arm when I tried to turn around to glance at the group again. "Not now," he said under his breath.

"That man was lying," I said, trying to wrench myself away. "They know something about Fausta. Let me go talk—"

"Keep walking." The force of his voice startled me.

"What . . ."

"Keep walking," he said again, and pulled me along at such a pace I couldn't catch my breath long enough to speak. Finally, when we had left the market square and the people were no longer in sight, he slowed our pace. I tried once again to protest.

"Why did you—"

"They know where she is, and so do I," he said, "but they still aren't sure they can trust you with the truth."

"If you know where she is, I demand you tell me now."

Father Colin gave me a look that was both surprise and amusement. "You demand?" he said.

"Tell me!" I thought he probably didn't like my demanding or my lack of humility, but I was certain by now that Fausta must be in trouble, and I wanted even more to help her. I half expected Father Colin to scold me for my impertinence. Instead he looked at me silently for a moment, then took my arm again, this time with more gentleness.

"Come," he said. "I'll do better than tell you; I'll show you."

"You knew all along where she was, didn't you?" I said, taking quick steps to keep up with him.

"Not until they told us."

"Told us?" I said, turning my head to look at him, still hurrying to keep up. "They told us nothing. Obviously they all know, even the little girl, but that man won't let them tell us."

"It's just that they can't be sure of what you would do. Or what I would do either, for that matter. But by their manner, they told us," the priest said. "Besides that, the child gave it away."

"I don't understand."

"You will soon enough," he said without looking at me. "And as I promised, I will show you where she is, but you must never try to find her again."

"But—"

"We're almost there." He held my arm with an even firmer grip. "Don't say anything. I will speak for both of us."

We were still only a short distance from the church, but we were in a part of town I'd never seen before. The street was lined with shacks, even poorer and more dilapidated than the worst of peasant hovels I'd seen or lived in. A few men were out on the street, but there were more women than men. There

seemed to be at least one or two women outside each of the little houses. They huddled together, wrapped in cloaks against
the cool autumn weather, except when a man was nearby. Then
they dropped their cloaks partway to reveal partially covered
breasts, or, in one case, completely bare breasts. Sometimes
they even showed a leg all the way up to the knee.

It didn't take long for someone to spot us, and as soon as
they did, all of the men and some of the women disappeared
into the shadows between the buildings or inside the hovels. I
knew by now that we were in the section of town designated
for *la prostituta*. Some of the women faced us brazenly.

"*Ciao, padre!*" one of them called. "Are you here in the
service of God or seeking my service?"

Her rude remark made the others around her laugh. One
of them coughed, reminding me of Fausta.

"I seek only your goodwill." Father Colin gave her his daz-
zling smile as he spoke those words and continued to walk toward her. I found myself holding back a little.

"Ha!" the woman said with a haughty toss of her head.
"My goodwill has nothing to do with it. If it's not my body you
want, then it's my soul. You can have either one for a price."

"I can offer you only my prayers." The words he spoke were
the words one would expect from a priest, but there was a little hint of laughter in his voice, as if he were flirting with her.

"Then take your business elsewhere, *padre*," she said, waving him away with a quick flip of her hand. "Your prayers

won't buy me a place to piss, much less food for me and my daughter."

She had a daughter! Somehow I was shocked by that, although common sense told me I shouldn't have been. I expected her to turn and walk away, but to my surprise she didn't. Instead she stood and watched as Father Colin walked toward her, as if that was exactly what she expected him to do.

"Are you well, Maria?"

Again I was surprised, this time to think that this coarse woman of the streets had the same name as the Holy Mother, but I was even more surprised that Father Colin seemed to know her so well, or that she knew him equally as well, judging by her next reaction.

She shrugged. "I'm well enough." She leaned toward him and spoke in a quiet voice. "But Beatricia is not. You must help her." She signaled toward one of the hovels with a movement of her head.

Father Colin, with a concerned look on his face, took a step toward the little shack, but he quickly turned back to look at me. "This is Margherita," he said. "See that no harm comes to her." With that he stepped inside the house.

"Why are you here?" Maria said, looking at me again. Her eyes took in everything about me, from the top of my head where I had inexpertly resecured my hair to the fine shoes I had put on my feet again to protect them against the cold.

"I came with the priest," I said, too unnerved to say more.

She continued to scrutinize me. "You're from the bath-houses." She was referring to the higher-quality prostitutes who plied their trade with men of more wealth and greater standing who frequented the bathhouses. "Or else you're one of those pious merchants' wives who wants to save our souls."

"I am neither." I tried to make my voice sound bolder than I felt. "I'm searching for someone. Her name is Fausta."

There was a change in Maria's expression, so slight it might not have been there at all. "What makes you think you'll find her here?"

"Father Colin thinks so," I said, growing a little bolder. "I must find her. I must make sure she's come to no harm. My husband banished her from his house, and she has nowhere to go. No way to feed herself."

Maria narrowed her eyes. "Ah, yes, just as I thought. You are indeed one of those pious merchants' wives. Your husband threw her out, did he? And now you want to make amends by saving her soul. Well, you needn't worry about Fausta. She has a way to feed herself. In fact, she's making herself a few *quat-trini* now," she added with a glance toward one of the little houses farther down the row.

Without thinking, I immediately walked toward the house. It was only when I heard the women laughing behind my back that I stopped, realizing that I had no idea what to do. The women's taunting confused me even more.

"Go on," Maria said. "Make it a threesome."

"But don't expect Fausta to share her fee with you," another said. That remark brought laughter from all of them.

"Maybe Fausta can teach you something that will please your husband," another said.

"Or maybe you'll like it and decide to join us," Maria added.

They went on with their taunting and their laughter while I stood there, still uncertain about what to do. I was about to turn and run away, giving them even more to laugh about, when the door to the little house opened and a man emerged, clad in only his hose and carrying his tunic over his arm in spite of the cold. In the next second a woman stepped out to throw the contents of a chamber pot on the street. She was dressed in a loose gown, open at the front, and her hair was unbound and falling to her shoulders. In spite of that, I recognized her immediately.

"Fausta?" My voice sounded timid and frightened, even to my own ears.

She turned to look at me where I stood frozen in place. "Bloody hell! It's you," she said just before she fled into the house.

"No, don't run," I cried after her as my feet finally loosened from the ground. "Fausta! Wait. Please." I was at her door before she was able to slam it shut. "Fausta," I said again, "I must talk to you."

"Go away, Lady Margherita. There's nothing here for you."

She coughed and pulled the open-front gown closed and clutched it with her fingers.

"*You* are here, Fausta. Please, I must talk to you." I managed to wedge myself inside. The room was small and dark and smelled of sweat and piss. There was a fireplace with a few dirty cooking pots scattered around it, a small table with one chair, and a pallet on the floor made of little more than rags that must have been her bed.

She turned her back to me and folded her arms over the loose gown. "I have nothing to say to you."

"Let me help you."

"You can't help. Now go." She threw the words at me over her shoulder.

"You don't have to do this, Fausta. I can—"

"What else can I do?" she asked, whirling around to face me. The fire of anger was in her eyes, and there were bruises on her face.

"Fausta, your face! Someone—"

"It happens to all of us," she said, cutting me off.

Certainly I was the last person on earth to argue with that. Still, I wanted to do something for her. "I can help," I said. "I can bring you food. I'll find clothes for you and blankets so you don't have to do this."

"No, you can't." Her voice was defiant. "If Master Vasari finds out, you'll once again have colors on your face to match mine. He could even toss you out to join me."

I tried to speak, but no words would come. She was right. There was a risk that I'd be caught, that I'd be beaten and forced to stop helping her, a chance even that I might find myself in her straits. It came to me suddenly and with great shock that there might be little else she could do than what she was doing. "A convent, maybe . . ." I was trying desperately to think of something.

"And where is there a convent that would take me? Me, with no dowry to secure my place." She coughed again, a loose rattling sound.

Again, I knew she was right.

"Oh, my lady . . ." She looked at me, shaking her head, and her voice had softened a little. "You mustn't worry about me. I'll find my way. And I'll not be here like this for long, I swear. With only a little more time and a little more gold, I'll have enough to buy a decent dress. Then I can present myself at the bathhouse, where the gentlemen are. They'll pay me more than the few *quattrini* I make here."

"No!" My voice cracked from the burden of tears I was trying to hold back. "This is not for you. You are a good woman; you—"

"Yes," she said. "I am as good as most, and I say again, you mustn't worry. 'Tis only the church that condemns me. See." She spread her hands to take in the squalor of the tiny room. "The town even sets aside a district for the likes of me. They say women like me are necessary—to feed the savage hunger of men, to keep them from raping fine women like you. They even collect taxes from me. So they need me in their own way as much as my customers do. And they'll like it even better when I move to the bathhouse and make more money so they can collect even more."

"But your immortal soul is—"

"I have no soul," she said with a laugh that sent her into a coughing fit. "Now go," she said, pushing me out while her face turned scarlet from the exertion of coughing. With one final push I was outside, and the door closed behind me. I stood there for a moment, not knowing what to do before I walked away, feeling helpless. Then I heard her call my name in a voice that was now hoarse from the coughing spasms.

I turned around to see her standing in the doorway, clutching her gown.

"They told me someone—a lady dressed in fine garments—left bread for them. Out by the market square. It was you, wasn't it?"

I looked at her, too surprised at what she'd said to be able to speak.

"Yes," she said. "It was you."

I tried again to say something, but before I could speak more than her name, a man approached wearing the rough tunic of a common laborer. Fausta called to him, then approached him, speaking to him in low tones and in words impossible for me to hear. She pulled him into her dark little room and once again closed the door.

Chapter 10

FAUSTA'S BRUISED FACE and the way she turned her back on me as she disappeared into that awful little house haunted my dreams that night, along with the little girl who had been struck down for something she'd said in innocence. I awoke the next morning feeling tired, but I was up and dressed and out of my room before Concetta, my new maid, arrived to help me.

"You didn't sleep well, signora." Rufina gave me a scrutinizing look as she kneaded the bread for Dominico's breakfast.

I answered her only with a shrug.

"Too soon to blame it on the babe," she added, frowning. "He's not yet big enough to rob your sleep with his kicking and beating his fists against your womb."

"You're probing, Rufina. You've no right to do that." I sat down on one of the stools in the corner near the fireplace and rested my head in both my hands while my elbows were propped on my knees. "But you're right," I added with a sigh and without looking up at her. "It's not the babe that keeps me awake. It's bad dreams." It was such a bother to try to keep her in her place the way Lorenzia had taught me. It was much easier to think of her as a friend.

"Bad dreams?" The alarm in Rufina's voice made me look up. "Dreams of what?"

"Of Fausta, and of . . . of others."

"Santa Maria, child, you mustn't do that." She made the sign of the cross, leaving a daub of flour on her forehead. "Such dreams could harm the babe. They could cause it to be born deformed."

"I have no control over my dreams, Rufina," I said with my weary voice, now edged a little with fear.

"Sleep with a crucifix under your pillow, and drink only the evening's milking of a goat before you go to bed." Rufina pointed a finger at me to emphasize her words. She reminded me once again of my mother, and I would not dare disobey her.

"Yes. Yes, of course I will," I said.

After a few seconds of silence she spoke again, looking up at me from her task. "And don't think of Fausta. She has found her way by now, I'm sure."

"No, she hasn't. I fear she is completely lost. I fear for her life."

Rufina stopped her kneading and looked at me with an expression of horror. "What are you saying, child?"

"She lives in one of the little houses on the street behind the church where the other women live—the ones who sell their bodies. I think the men beat her sometimes, and she is thin, as if she doesn't have enough to eat. And I fear her cough is—"

Rufina cut me off with her sharp voice. "How do you know this?"

"I've seen her."

"You've seen her? You've been to the district? *Santa Madre!*" She crossed herself once more. "You must never do that again."

"But she needs help," I said, sitting up straighter. "If I can bring her food and something warm to wear, maybe she won't have to—"

"No," Rufina said with such urgency it frightened me. She left the soft mound of dough on the table and walked to me with a few quick steps. "No," she said again, lifting me by my arms to a standing position and forcing me to look into her eyes. "If the master finds out you are seeing her, or even that you go to such places without seeing her, he will beat you. You must not do that," she said, emphasizing each word.

"Rufina, I—"

"And you'd best not let yourself be seen in the kitchen," she said, looking over her shoulder. I knew she was looking for Concetta; she trusted her no more than I did. "The master has complained about the amount of time you spend down here with us."

She was right. Dominico had, at first, paid little attention to exactly where in the house I spent my time. Lately, though, he'd been asking me about my visits to the kitchen. For a while I'd gotten by with the lie that I was simply overseeing the preparation of the food for the household, but he'd become more and more suspicious and had even insisted that I not go to the kitchen at all. Rufina and I both, as well as Grimani, suspected that Concetta was spying on me and reporting my movements to Dominico. It was not until her arrival in the household that Dominico had even noticed I'd ever been to the kitchen.

"You're right. It's best I go." My voice sounded tired, even to my own ears, and I moved away from Rufina with no zest in my steps.

"Remember what I said about not seeing Fausta." Rufina spoke in a hushed, urgent tone.

"I'll remember," I said without turning around to look at her. On my way out I stole a basket from a stack against the wall while Rufina was preoccupied with her work. I barely made it back to my room and scarcely had time to hide the basket under the bed before Concetta showed up.

"Up and dressed already, are you?" she said as she opened the door. "I never knew the wife of a gentleman—a true lady, that is—to do such a thing."

"No, I suppose not," I said with little interest. I knew she was trying to insult me by implying that I fell short of the mark of a true lady, but I felt no injury. After all, I was no lady; the role had been forced upon me. And besides, I had other more pressing concerns to think about. I couldn't stop worrying about Fausta's plight or how hungry and frightened the poor beggars near the marketplace gate were.

Concetta went on fussing around me, insisting that she rearrange my hair and that my lips be colored with red powder, my dress brushed with a damp cloth, my shoes cleaned and polished. It took all the patience I could muster to allow her to groom me, and even more to endure a breakfast with Dominico. Lorenzia, I learned, was still abed, and I was grateful for that small mercy.

Dominico and I spoke little during breakfast, since he seemed as preoccupied as I was. He had even brought a document of some sort to the table with him, and he kept running the tip of his knife down a column of what I think must have been numbers and moving his lips as if he were counting to himself. I think he asked me once about my visits to the kitchen, and I suppose I must have answered him satisfactorily, since he never looked up from his rows of numbers, and presently he stood, wiped his mouth with his sleeve, and left without another word.

I took that as my opportunity to hurry away as well, and, after I had taken as much of the leftover food as I could bundle in the skirt of my overdress, I hurried to my room and prepared myself to go out. I wore my shoes and the cloak Dominico expected me to wear when I went out, but underneath I wore an old rag of a dress I'd found in the kitchen the day before. It was an almost colorless gray and must have been something Rufina had discarded with the intent of using it as a kitchen rag.

After I'd placed the food in the basket, I hurried out of the
house and along the streets, trying to ignore the cold rain that
was about to become ice pellets. I was certain no one had seen
me leave, but even if they had, it was well-known among the
household that I had permission to go to church daily. Just before I reached the marketplace, I removed my shoes, wrapped
them in my cloak, and stored the bundle behind an old broken
stone that looked as if it might have once been part of a building. Of course, I was shivering, and I had forgotten the painful
cold of damp winter earth beneath my bare feet. A relentless
breeze sank sharp teeth into my skin. I tried to think, not of the
cold, but to summon a vision of my two Marys as I hurried toward the place in the square where I had found the people earlier. No vision would come to me, but I was trying so hard that,
for a moment at least, I forgot about my cold feet and the raw
sting of ice and wind on my arms.

The wide expanse of the market square spread out before
me, damp and gray as clabbered milk. Above me the heavy sky
made the icy rain look dark. There was no sign of life. Until I
saw a white vapor rising from behind a small structure before
it was swallowed by the gloom. I walked toward it and soon
saw that the vapor was smoke from a small fire, smoldering in
the dampness. Several people huddled around the embers,
wrapped in rags and tattered cloaks. I hurried toward them,
eager for whatever warmth I could get from the stingy fire.

Heads turned toward me as I drew closer, but no one hurried away from me this time. Either the cold had rendered them too miserable to move, or they no longer feared or distrusted me. Eyes that were haunted, desolate pools watched me as I approached. I thrust the basket forward.

"Here," I said. "I've brought more food."

All eyes were on the basket now, and some of the people moved toward me, but they all stopped at the sound of the voice of the man who had challenged me before.

"What do you want from us?" he asked.

"Only that you will take this," I answered, pushing the basket forward again.

"Why do you dress as you do?" He sounded angry. Or at least suspicious.

"To show my humil—"

"Can't you see she's a holy woman? A saint, maybe," someone said before I could finish my answer.

"No," I said, shaking my head. "I'm neither holy nor saintly. I'm a sinner, just as you are, but our Heavenly Father asks no less of me than that I share what I have with those who have nothing." I pulled a loaf of bread from the basket and, with the handle still over my arm, broke the bread and handed it to those around me. I regretted that I had only table scraps to offer. Before I could hand out all of it, someone slipped the basket from my arm and he, along with all of the others, ravaged its contents, reminding me of the hungry swine I had fed at home.

The man who had first spoken to me, the one called Benno, didn't join the others. Instead he continued to look at me.

"I am Margherita," I said, attempting to break the awkward silence between us.

"I know your name," he said. "Father Colin told me, remember?"

"So he did," I said. "Have you seen him again?" I hadn't admitted to myself until that moment how much I'd hoped to see him again myself.

"He comes to us often," he said. "He brought us these blankets," he said, pointing to the rags on the backs of the others, "and this bit of wood."

"Have you seen him today?" I asked.

The man shrugged. "He comes when he can," he said, as if that were an answer. He continued to look at me for a moment before he spoke. "I'm called Benno."

"I know. I've heard the others call you by that name. And the child?" I nodded toward the little girl whose mother had struck her.

"Balbina," he said. "And her mother is Pippa."

Both mother and daughter were too occupied with trying to fill their mouths to hear their names spoken.

I pointed to the basket that was now being passed from person to person. "You need to eat some of the food I brought."

"I'll eat when the others have finished," he said. "I want to make sure there's enough."

"Oh, there will be enough," I said, "with some left over." I don't know what made me say that. The words were out of my mouth before I knew they were coming. I had the indescribably odd sensation that the Holy Mother had used my mouth to speak her words.

I had little time to ponder that, however. I had to retrieve my basket, leave the market square, and hurry back to where I'd hidden my clothes and put on my cloak and shoes in time to enter the house before I was missed. I thought I had accomplished just that when I was able to slip inside and make my way halfway up the stairs before I heard Dominico's voice behind me.

"Margherita!"

I stopped and stood dead still without turning around. The sound of his heavy boots on the stairs filled me with dread. His hand on my shoulder was a claw, light and bony, piercing my flesh. He used it, leverlike, to force me to turn and face him.

"Where have you been, wife?"

His words were spoken blandly enough, but the November cold in his eyes made me stammer. "I . . . I've been out. Ministering to the poor," I added when I saw his gaze fall to the basket on my arm.

"Ministering? How?" His tone had already condemned me.

"I took food to the hungry, sir, and—"

"You stole food from my table?"

"Oh, no, sir. I took only the scraps." I hated the frightened sounds I was making.

"You took food from my table. Concetta saw you. And I suppose you met with that new priest again. Shameless woman! You, with your belly already advancing before you, dallying with a man of God."

"Oh, no, sir!" I said again. "I have never—"

The back of his hand slammed my face, his hard knuckles boring into my right eye. "You will minister to the poor only at my direction, and you will stay away from all priests."

"But who will hear my confession? I must—"

He raised his hand again, as if to strike me, making me cringe away from him. "I will hear your confession, wench. You will describe your dalliances to me in detail." With that he dropped his hand without striking me, and, with a final surprisingly sad look, he breathed my name—"Ah, Margherita"— and shook his head before he turned away and walked down the stairs. I hurried to my room and refused to allow Concetta in to bring me my supper. I knew I should feel ashamed for displeasing my husband, but I felt nothing but anger. My anger turned to worry for Fausta and Benno and the others, and finally to despair because I felt helpless.

Again I slept very little, partly because the bruise under my eye was throbbing and partly because of my despair. I stayed in my room the next morning long past the time for breakfast, grateful that Concetta had not come to inform me that the master wanted me to join him at his table. I passed the next two days without coming out of my room and without repast. I had sunk deeper and deeper into depression because I was being forced to live with a man I could not love and whose brutality frightened me, but most of all because I couldn't help those who so desperately needed my help.

Concetta came to my door daily, and daily I sent her away. No one else came. Rufina and Grimani must have been afraid, and Lorenzia, no doubt, was happy not to have to contend with me. Dominico's normal habits were to ignore me for days until he wanted to try to bed me or wanted me to accompany him somewhere. Finally on the third night I slept a little, but it was fitful sleep that provided no rest. While it was still dark, I was awakened suddenly by a strange light in my window. I was weak from want of both food and sleep, but I managed to rise enough to rest my weight on my left elbow while I stared at the light. A weak cry of relief and delight escaped my throat when I saw that it was the Holy Mother. She was speaking in the voice of my own mother, it seemed.

"Don't forsake them," she said. "They need you."

"Mother?" I said in my small, feeble voice. "Mother, is that you?" I don't know to this day whether I was asking for my own mother or for the Virgin, but I couldn't forget the words she spoke—*Don't forsake them. They need you.*

I got out of bed, feeling dazed and not quite myself, and

walked toward the window, half expecting her to disappear, but she remained—the Holy Mother, bathed in light and reassuring me with her smile. *Don't forsake them,* she said again before she disappeared into the light.

I stood transfixed for a moment before I turned away from the window to get dressed once again in the rag I'd found. I wore my good cloak over the dress as I went with my basket on my arm to the kitchen. I had no idea the time of day, but it must have been sometime between matins and lauds, because the sky was still dark and neither Grimani nor Rufina had yet entered the kitchen. I took what I needed—bread, some meats, turnips, and a candle to help light my path—and left the house. I made my way first to the church, because I wanted to thank the Holy Mother for appearing to me.

I had scarcely bent my knees to pray in the Virgin's chapel when I heard a noise behind me. I stopped my meditation almost before it had begun and turned around to look. It was Father Colin I saw. He had just come into the church, I suppose for his own prayers. Remembering my husband's warning about not speaking even to a priest and not ministering to the poor, I felt suddenly overwhelmed with despair. It must have shown on my face, even in the darkened church lit only by candle.

"Signora Vasari?" he said, and walked toward me. By now I was standing, not certain whether or not to flee. All I could do, however, was remain immobile. When he was close enough to see my face, he gasped. "Margherita!" His voice was full of alarm.

For a moment everything went black, and I felt as if my body were spiraling downward, perhaps to hell, but I sensed his hands and arms stop the fall.

"*Santa Madre!* What has happened to you?" He picked me up in his arms and carried me away. I must have fainted again, because the next thing I remembered, I was in a small room on a narrow bed. A monk's cell. Father Colin's room. He was kneeling beside the bed with his arm under my head, holding a cup of water with his other hand.

A strange, alien cry escaped my throat as I tried to push his hand away and get myself out of the bed. If anyone found me here and told Dominico, he would kill us both. My long fast had left me weak, though, and it took little effort for Father Colin to restrain me.

"Your face," he said as he laid me back with a gentleness I had never experienced. "Someone hit you. Did your husband . . . ?"

I didn't answer his unfinished question. How could I? I had been warned not to, and besides, it took too much effort to summon my voice.

The next thing I remember was the warm broth he held at my mouth and encouraged me to drink. It was salty and had a strong taste. It took me a moment to realize it was the broth of beef, since, though I had eaten the meat of cattle a few times in my new life, I still was not accustomed to its taste. He gave me wine and dark bread that I had to soak in the wine to soften before I could chew it.

I was surprised at how quickly my strength returned and the lightness of my head righted itself to its normal weight. I sat up in bed staring at him, feeling the bruise under my eye throb. Father Colin sat in the room's only chair a few feet away.

He spoke one word. "Why?"

"I displeased him. By taking food from his table to give to the poor, food that would have been thrown to the dogs." I was surprised at the anger and resentment in my voice. "He has forbidden me to return to them, and he's forbidden me to speak to you."

"So you have defied him on both counts."

"Yes," I said. "I confess that I have defied my husband on both counts." I took a moment to gather my courage. "But I must also confess that I do not seek forgiveness for those sins. I will do it again."

Something flickered in his eyes, but it was quickly gone, and he spoke not a word. His silence made me uncomfortable, but I refused to let go of my resolve. Finally, after several seconds, he spoke.

"Your kindness and your courage outshine even your considerable physical beauty," he said. "They do, in fact, make you more beautiful." He had a strange way of speaking, with his accent chiseled from the cold islands to the north. It took me a moment to realize that he had given me a compliment. Belatedly, I blushed, which made him laugh.

"Ah, your color returns. The broth does its job with haste."

"And I must leave with haste," I said, trying, with success this time, to get out of bed. The moment I stood, I saw the blackness again and felt myself sway. Father Colin was on his feet immediately, holding my arms, forcing me down on the bed.

"You need more time. I suspect you haven't eaten in a while. Why?"

"I could not," I said. "For worry of them that have no food."

"Foolishness! Depriving yourself of food helps no one."

"But the saints, the holy ones, fast regularly to bring themselves closer to God."

"Foolishness," he said again. "There are better ways to approach God. And besides, you must think of your babe. Think of your husband's anger if he learns you've starved yourself and in so doing deprived his offspring."

"The babe is not his," I said with a bitter laugh. That was one sin I had never confessed to a priest, and, to make matters worse for my own soul, at that moment I was not ashamed of either the sin or the failure to confess. If my head had been clearer, I might have thought that the devil had taken possession of my soul. I told him the story of Augustino and me.

Father Colin said nothing.

"You condemn me," I said, full of remorse.

"I have no power to condemn," he said. "I cannot even tell you that God condemns you."

"Surely you know he condemns a fornicator."

"I don't know that in every case he does. I know only that our Lord knows what is in your heart and under what circumstances you may have coupled with your lover. I know, also, that God made woman to bear children and that our Lord, himself, was born of a woman."

"But I am a mere mortal. Not the mother of God."

"Nevertheless, didn't you tell me you thought of this young man, Augustino, as your betrothed? Perhaps God thought so as well. Perhaps it is Augustino who has done the greater wrong by failing to declare himself for you at the crucial moment."

I was stunned. "Then I have not sinned?"

"I cannot say, signora. That is between you and God. However, as a priest, I must remind you of the commandments and warn you to obey them always. For a woman as beautiful as you, it will not always be easy."

I must confess that although a part of me still felt the need to repent, I was very much pleased by the thought that he had twice called me beautiful, but all I said was, "Yes, Father."

"What I said before is still true, though," he said. "You must not harm yourself with too much fasting, for it harms the babe as well. Remember, God has entrusted you to hold and nurture this growing soul. You must do your best for the babe, and for God as well."

"Yes, Father," I said again.

"Perhaps, also, you should leave ministering to the poor to others if your husband punishes you for—"

"I can't do that, Father."

There was a look of alarm in his eyes. "Margherita, don't you understand how dangerous this can be for you?"

"Don't you understand that I must do what I can?" I stood up again, this time with more success. I wanted to tell him the words I'd heard in my vision—the Holy Mother saying, *Don't forsake them. They need you*—but while I was struggling for the right words, he spoke again.

"Do you want to end up like Beatricia?" His voice was angry, scolding.

I remembered that was the name of the woman in the district of *la prostituta* who the woman called Maria had said was ill and sent Father Colin in to see her.

"What does she have to do with me?" I sounded defiant, but I was determined that no one would keep me from helping those I knew needed my help.

He looked at me for a moment, his expression grave. "She was beaten," he said, sounding both sad and weary. "By a man whom I suppose she must have displeased," he added. "I buried her last night."

The expression on his face was so full of grief and despair, I couldn't speak. I could only manage a gasp.

"I must go," I said at length, and gathered up my basket of food and my cloak.

"Yes," he said, "you must."

When I turned to look at him, there were tears in his eyes.

After I had shed my cloak and my shoes, I made my way to the market square, where this time I was greeted with eager kindness as well as concern for my bruised face. It might have lifted my spirits greatly had I been able to stop thinking of a woman I'd never met dying from the wounds she'd suffered in a beating. The same thing could happen to Fausta if I didn't find a way to help her.

By the time I retrieved my cloak and shoes and returned home later that day, I had a plan. I could only hope that Fausta was right when she said things would be better if she could work among the gentlemen who frequented the bathhouses. Certainly not every gentleman would be as brutal as my own husband. I would provide her with a dress fine enough to be seen at the bathhouses, and I would pray that she was right about it being safer there.

Chapter 11

A FEW DAYS LATER I finally had the opportunity to leave Dominico's house long enough to go to Fausta. It was a day I knew he would be meeting with other merchants concerning the sale of goods to the French. He was away from home and his office for several hours.

I had become quite skillful at getting out of the house with my basket of food before even the servants were up and then returning unnoticed. At least I was not noticed by Concetta or Lorenzia or Dominico. Grimani and Rufina knew I slipped into the house through the kitchen—something I was no longer reluctant to do, since I knew they would now respond to my knock on the locked back door. Rufina always gave me a warning look and shook her head in dismay. Grimani kept a watch for anyone who might be coming down the stairs and signaled me with his eyes or with what others would think was a careless clank of his knife on the big iron pot if I was in danger of being caught.

On the day I went to Fausta, I left by the front door in clear view of Concetta. I thanked God that Lorenzia was still in bed. I was dressed quite properly in one of the dresses that had been made to accommodate my expanding belly, and I wore my good cloak. Concetta had even helped me dress. I made no mention to her about where I was going. I had no doubt that she knew Dominico had forbidden me to minister to the poor and told me to stay away from priests. Even if I told her I was going to church to pray, she would tell Dominico, so I made no mention of where I was going.

After she left my room I took one of my other dresses—one of the smaller ones that would be a better fit for Fausta—and concealed it under my cloak before I passed by her on my way out.

When I arrived at the street of little houses, there were no women standing outside to greet me this time. I assumed it was because the weather had grown colder. It was too cold to have windows open, certainly. Yet some of the women had opened them to stand where potential customers could see them. Most of them were bundled in heavy wraps, but a few shivered in nothing but the skimpy attire of their trade.

I made my way to Fausta's house and found both the door and the window closed. Did that mean she was entertaining a customer? Or did it mean she was simply protecting herself against the cold? I stood outside for several seconds, not knowing what to do. I heard her cough more than once, but there were no other sounds from inside. Finally I knocked at her door.

Almost instantly the door opened. I gasped at what I saw.

It was Fausta standing in front of me in the same dirty dress she'd worn the last time I saw her. She was thinner, and the skin covering her sunken cheeks and stringy throat was a sallow gray.

"Madam Vasari!"

"Margherita," I said, correcting her.

"Go away!" She tried to close the door, but I brought my foot forward, stopping it. "Go away!" she said again. "You shouldn't be here. I told you, if Master Vasari saw you—"

"He's busy today. He's not going to see me." I managed to force my way inside by pushing Fausta aside. She seemed to weigh no more than a feather.

She tried to speak, perhaps to protest more, but she was seized by a fit of coughing and could say nothing at all. Finally she spit a glob of blood into a bucket, then sat down heavily on the bed, exhausted. Her face looked even more colorless than before, and she was gasping for breath.

"Oh, Fausta," I said, sitting beside her and taking her into my arms. "You aren't well. You must get more rest, and next time I'll have Rufina make you a poultice for your chest to stop that cough."

"Bah! Rufina's poultices stink, and they do no good. She gave me plenty when I was at your house."

"Hush now," I said, scolding her as if she were a child. "Your cough was never this bad when you were with us, so they must have done some good."

Her only response was another, "Bah!"

"You're too thin, Fausta. I should have brought food as well."

This time she only looked at me with her hollow eyes without responding at all.

"I have no food with me, but I did bring something." As I spoke I stood up, pulled the dress from inside my cloak, and let it unfold to its full length.

Fausta looked at the dress, and then at me, her eyes wide and questioning.

"It's for you," I said. "So you can work at the bathhouses."

She still didn't speak, but she continued to look at the dress and then at me while tears filled her eyes. Finally she rose from the bed and fell to her knees in front of me, bending over to kiss my feet. "You are a saint, Margherita, an angel and a saint."

"Stand up, Fausta," I said, embarrassed. Taking her arm, I pulled her up to face me. "I'm no angel and no saint. If I were, I'd find a way to help you so you wouldn't have to work at this dreadful trade at all."

"A saint," she said over and over again. "A true saint. How can I ever repay you?"

"There's no need—"

"Oh, yes!" She turned away from me and bustled toward the fireplace where a pottage steamed over the fire. She pulled a bowl and a ladle from a shelf above the hearth. When she dipped the ladle into the pot I could hear it scraping the bottom and knew that there must be precious little in there. It took several dips to half fill the bowl. "Here, take this." She shoved the dish of pottage toward me. "It will warm your insides and keep you warm all the way home."

I took the bowl and hesitated a moment. It was all she had, I knew. I didn't want to take her last drop of food, but she looked at me with such eagerness that I dared not insult her by refusing to eat. I tipped the bowl to my mouth to drink the way I'd learned to do at home because we had none of the fancy spoons I'd become accustomed to in Dominico's house.

The gruel was watery, with only a few leeks and turnips to give it substance. I took a small sip and handed the bowl back to Fausta. "Join me," I said, trying to smile. "We will have a celebration."

Fausta hesitated only a short moment before she took the bowl with an eagerness that surprised me and drank some of the contents. I was glad to see that the dress had at least served to stir her appetite. When she handed the bowl back to me I shook my head and touched my stomach. "I can hold no more. The babe will only send it back up through my mouth again."

"Ah, the babe," Fausta said with a little laugh that made her cough again. "Vasari struts like a peacock because he thinks everyone believes he's got you with child so quick."

"How do you know this?" I asked.

"Oh, I hear many voices," she said, taking another sip of

the pottage. "You'd be surprised at the number I hear, and how they all speak of everyone's private affairs. Even yours, my little angel. I know how you and the young priest go among the poor. I'm surprised Vasari doesn't stop you."

"I do no harm," I said, although I didn't want to admit to her that Dominico had, indeed, tried to stop me.

She shrugged. "It matters not whether you do harm or good. He owns you. He can do with you as he wishes." She laughed. "Well, perhaps not everything he wishes, as some of us well know."

"What are you talking about?" It alarmed me to think that she might be implying that others knew of Dominico's physical impairment and would therefore know that the baby was not his. If anyone dared insinuate differently, he would surely fly into a rage and beat me.

"Remember, signora, I know about Vasari's limp twig, same as you. And he beat me, same as you, for not turning that twig to hard wood." Fausta was holding the dress against her body and looking down to admire it as she spoke.

"No one else knows, do they?"

Fausta's little laugh turned to a cough again. "Only those he's tried to bed, I'd say, and who knows how many that is?" She glanced up at me. "Probably not many, since he wouldn't want to embarrass himself. And I'm no fool, signora. I haven't told a soul. I know how dangerous that could be for you."

Without knowing I was going to, I burst into tears—

something that, as I said, happened more often now that I was with child. It was the idea of so many of us being in danger that made me weep. I was perhaps endangered very little compared to Fausta and the poor who lived near the market square and all the women in the little hovels.

A look of alarm took over Fausta's face when she saw my tears. She threw the dress on the bed and reached her thin arms toward me. "No, no, you mustn't cry." She led me to the bed and forced me to sit on the edge. "He won't find out you've been here. And if he ever harms you, he'll have me to answer to."

I shook my head. "It's not me; it's . . . it's everyone. You, poor Beatricia, everyone who . . . Beatricia's dead," I said, sobbing even harder. "Did you know that? Father Colin buried her in a pauper's grave. Someone beat her until she died." I went on sobbing even harder.

"Now, now, you mustn't do that. You must remain cheerful for the sake of the child." Fausta had become the mother now as she sat with one arm over my shaking shoulders. "Doesn't Rufina tell you how this is bad for you and how it can mark the babe? And you mustn't worry about Beatricia. Father Colin absolved her of her sins before she died, and the one what done it to her died without absolution. We seen to that."

A chill that had nothing to do with the weather and the drafty little house gripped me. "What do you mean?" I asked.

"I mean he's dead," Fausta said.

"But did you . . . ?"

"Don't ask too many questions. Just know we have our ways, and we take care of our own."

"Fausta!"

She smiled. "Maria was a midwife once. You know her, I think. She said she talked to you that first time you came with the priest. She takes care of all of us with her herbs and potions. Poor thing is no longer allowed to midwife because of a certain merchant's wife who died with the childbed sickness, but Maria still remembers her medicines. Why, she even has some that have no taste when they're mixed with wine."

"Oh, Mother of God," I said, feeling sick. "I hope you're not saying she gave him—"

"Now don't you fret," Fausta said, rubbing my shoulders as she talked. "He died of apoplexy. One of his guild brothers saw him grip his chest, and the breath went out of him. Old Death has taken many a man that same way. Nothing unusual about that."

When I could finally speak, I could manage only a whisper. "Fausta, you must get away from here. You must use that dress and go to the bathhouses tomorrow."

"Don't worry about me." She pulled me to my feet. "But you'd best be getting home now. I've plenty of work to do myself." She picked up the dress and held it next to her body one more time before she ushered me to the door. I could hear her coughing as I left. On my way home I prayed that I had done the right thing by giving her the dress.

Seeing Fausta in the condition she was in troubled me more than I realized, and I felt drawn to the Virgin's chapel again. I prayed for a long time, or rather I knelt at her feet without forming any words with my tongue or even in my mind. I simply let her love and kindness surround and comfort me. When I arose and turned around I saw Father Colin standing a few feet away near a window glowing with sunlight so that he looked as if he were bathed in the light of heaven. He smiled and held out his hand as if he'd been waiting for me. The tranquillity I'd received from the Virgin still filled and surrounded me so that it seemed only natural that I return his smile and reach my hand to join his.

"You are faithful in your prayers, and your faithfulness makes you lovely," he said, holding my hand and looking into my eyes.

I felt myself blush and dropped my eyes. "Father Colin, you shouldn't—"

"I know; I shouldn't say such things to you," he said. "And I pray that you, as well as God, will forgive me."

"I was going to say you shouldn't speak to me at all. Remember, my husband has forbidden me to speak to you."

"And you have vowed to defy him."

"May God forgive me," I said, dropping my eyes again. "I am made wretched by my disobedience, which I refuse to recant. I mean, I *should* be made wretched. But I'm not. I'm filled with happiness. The Holy Mother has appeared to me in a vision. Twice."

Father Colin gave me a surprised look. "You are indeed blessed," he said, and to my surprise he actually bowed to me as if I were a bishop or a saint or some other kind of holy person. "She had a message for you?" he asked, facing me again.

"She told me not to forget them. She said they needed me. Do you think she meant the poor? I feel that is what she meant."

"Yes," he said, "because that is what you want it to mean."

His words puzzled me. "No, you don't understand. It's not a matter of what I think. It's a matter of God's will."

He chuckled, and at first I thought it was some foolish mistake I'd made that caused him to do that. "You're right, of course. The innocent always are. 'Out of the mouths of babes . . .' "

"What?" I asked, puzzled again.

"Never mind," he said, and, still holding my hand, he pulled me toward a door at the side of the church. "Come with me. I want to show you something." He'd let go of my hand, but he held my arm in a solicitous manner as we made our way through the door down a flight of stairs leading somewhere below the sanctuary.

"Where are we going?" I asked as we reached the bottom of the stairs. "What is it that you will show me?"

The excitement in my voice made him laugh again. "Don't be so impatient. Now close your eyes."

His playful tone made me laugh this time, and I laughed even harder when I bumped my nose on a wall.

"Careful," he said.

"You're the one who has to be careful. I can't see with my eyes closed, you know."

We both laughed, giddy with the delicious tension that moved like sparks of lightning between us.

"Here," he said, taking my hand again. "Come this way. And stop peeking. I haven't told you to open your eyes yet."

"I'm not peeking."

"I saw you open your eyes."

"No, I didn't."

"Would you lie to a priest?"

"Well, only a little lie," I said, which made us both laugh again. We were still laughing as he placed his hand over my eyes and his other arm around my shoulders to lead me away from the wall and several steps beyond. I could hardly concentrate on walking, since all I could think about was how strong his arm that surrounded me felt and how his long, sensuous fingers caressed my face. That distraction served only to make me stumble again and to giggle at my awkwardness.

Finally he stopped. "All right," he said. "You can look now." His arm tightened around me for the briefest of seconds before he dropped his hand from my eyes and then from my shoulders.

It took a moment for my eyes to adjust and for me to confirm what my nose had detected a few seconds earlier—the smell of fresh-cut wood. We were in a room resembling a carpenter shop with saws and hammers on benches, along with a few slabs of wood in hues of gold and brown and red, and sawdust on the floor showing a crisscrossing trail of footprints.

"It's my workshop," he said, as if he'd sensed my confusion.

"You're a carpenter?"

"Not by trade, of course. It's only a diversion for me. My skills are weak, but they are sufficient for me to construct a few poor hovels as protection against the coming winter for our friends near the market square."

"They—all of us—are blessed to have you among us," I said, sobered by his goodness.

"Flattery will get you nothing," he said, sounding flippant again as he moved away from me. "And I didn't bring you here to talk about my good works." He walked toward a cloth-covered mound in the corner of the room. "This," he said, "is for you." He made an elaborate gesture of pulling the cloth away to reveal what was underneath.

It was the most beautiful cradle I'd ever seen, not rough-hewn and splintery as my little brother Bernardino's was. This one was smooth and polished to a high sheen, and I could see a simple but beautiful carving of an angel at the head.

I was too overcome to speak. All I could do was clasp both of my hands to my mouth and breathe in an audible shriek of surprise. I looked at him, my open mouth still covered with my hands. Had he really said it was for me?

"For you," he said again. "For your baby."

I still couldn't speak.

"Don't you like it?"

"It . . . it's the most beautiful thing I've ever seen," I said finally, in little more than a whisper. I reached to touch it, tentatively at first, with only the tips of my fingers. It was not at all like touching wood. It was more like silk—the finest of silk, so soft I rubbed it with my palms and knelt to touch my face to it and to take in the sweet smell of the wood.

"It's too heavy for you to carry," he said. "I will have it sent to your house."

His words, spoken in kindness, brought me out of my lovely spell and filled me with fear. Dominico would be furious, and how could I explain the gift or that I had disobeyed him by speaking to Father Colin?

"You are afraid of what your husband will do," Father Colin said.

"You know that I have disobeyed him by coming here and by speaking to you. How can I . . ."

"You will tell him it is a gift from the bishop."

Surprise at his words kept me silent for a few seconds. "Lie to him?" I said when I could finally speak.

"It is not a lie."

"But . . ."

"The bishop is a friend of your husband's, as I'm sure you know. He wishes to acknowledge his best wishes for your husband's good fortune of having his wife pregnant."

"How do you know this?"

"Your parish priest who allows me to serve under him, Father Venantious, has communicated with the bishop. He suggested to his holiness that I craft a gift to be presented to Vasari in the name of the most reverend Bishop Fiorentino."

I studied Father Colin's face. "You don't lie with much grace," I said.

"It's true, I swear."

"Perhaps, but I sense your machinations. It's my guess that it was you who planted the idea in the mind of Father Venantious to contact the bishop."

"You are overly suspicious, madam. And what does it matter if you are right? It's still a gift from the most reverend father."

It was on the tip of my tongue to tell him not to send the cradle to Dominico's house, but when my eyes fell upon its beauty, and I imagined my baby sleeping peacefully in its confines, I couldn't speak for a moment.

"Make certain it's clear that it is a gift from the bishop," I said finally.

When the cradle arrived, Dominico was beside himself with pride and delight, and he ordered it placed, not in my bedroom as I had hoped, but in one of the *salas* where he received visitors so all could witness the honor that had been bestowed upon him by the bishop.

The arrival of the gift was the only thing that could bring him from his work. He was still busy with his talks regarding French markets. At least his distraction afforded me a little freedom. In the next few days I was able to see Benno and the group several times. Father Colin and I often went together to the market square where the poor gathered. Each time I managed to take a little food. I was no longer a suspicious stranger among them. Instead they welcomed me, and called me Margherita the Barefooted. Sometimes they even joked with me and teased me because my second toe on each foot was longer than my great toe. Benno said that was a sign of a strong body and a strong mind. Father Colin laughed when he heard that, and told me Benno was just trying to say I was stubborn.

We laughed a lot in those days, and when I was away from him I counted the hours until I would see him again. He made me feel safe. And happy. And loved, although I tried for a long time to convince myself it was the innocent love a woman would have for a friend.

The only thing that kept me from being completely happy was a nagging concern about Fausta.

I'd tried to visit her again, but there was no answer to my knock. Perhaps she had moved to the bathhouses, but I couldn't go there unaccompanied by Lorenzia. And even in her company I would risk shame bathing in my current condition.

Pippa worried that going barefooted in the cold of winter would cause me to have the grippe and would be bad for my baby. I told her the Holy Mother would protect me, and, to tell the truth, I no longer felt the cold on my feet. It was as if I'd regained the strength against the cold I'd had as a peasant girl. I could have, I suppose, gone back to wearing shoes, if not my silk dresses, when I visited the poor, but I had come to think of my bare feet as a badge of my acceptance among them, and, if truth be told, I believe they felt the same.

"You have become a saint to them," Father Colin said to me one day as we were walking back to the church from the market area. He had spent the day helping them build crude shelters with wood from his shop, and I had once again brought food.

I laughed. "I'm no saint. I'm only a sinner as you well know."

He reached for both my hands and brought me around to face him. "Your face is as lovely as the light of heaven when you laugh like that," he said. His words and his blue eyes, dancing in his face, so young and strong, once again gave me a feeling of giddy happiness. Our gazes held, and something passed between us, something that was at once wonderful and terrible, something we both knew we could not possess but that we could no longer deny.

"Margherita," he whispered, and held my gaze a moment longer before he let go of my hands. We walked in silence away from the market square. When we reached the intersection of streets where I would normally turn away to go home, I kept walking toward the church. I'd gone from contented happiness to feeling miserable, as if I had done something terribly wrong. I had a deep desire to talk to my saints, to somehow rid myself of the burden I didn't understand.

"You must go home now, Signora Vasari," Father Colin said when he saw that I was continuing on with him. I had grown so accustomed of late to his using my Christian name that the more formal address he used sounded foreign to me.

"I'm going to church to pray." My voice was tight, even angry-sounding, and I didn't know why. My emotions were like foreign demons roiling inside me. He said nothing in reply, and by the time we reached the church I felt even more unsettled, especially when we entered the vast cavern that was the sanctuary. Father Colin walked away from me as we entered. It was cold and damp inside. The altar loomed at the end of the cavern like a tired beast weighted down with a god's blood and body. I wanted to turn and run as if it were the devil and not the holy sacraments threatening me. Instead, I called out to Father Colin's back, "Hear my confession."

He stopped with his back still turned to me and stayed that way for a second or two before he turned around slowly to face me. "I cannot hear your confession." His voice was low and heavy, as if it, too, were weighted down with the blood and flesh of shame.

"Of course you can. You're a priest, aren't you?" Anger was creeping into my voice.

"I cannot hear your confession," he said again, with more firmness this time. Then he added, "Your sin is my sin." His gaze held mine for several seconds.

"You know nothing of my sins! How could you, when you refuse to listen to me?" I wouldn't allow myself to cry, but I couldn't keep my voice from breaking.

"Father Venantious will hear your confession. He will be here before vespers, as you know." His voice was cold, but his eyes—oh, those eyes—were blue-hot flames.

"*You* will hear it," I said, taking a step toward him. "*You* will hear that I have encouraged Fausta in the most mortal of sins by giving her a fine gown so she can continue her work as a prostitute among gentlemen rather than with filthy laborers. *You* will hear that I regularly steal food from my husband's kitchen, and—"

"Margherita, stop. This is not the way for you to—"

"No, I won't stop," I cried, placing my hand on his arm none too gently. "You will hear it all. You will hear that I love you and long for you in a manner that is doubly wrong because I am another's wife and you are wed to the—"

"Stop!" His shout echoed through the cavern, a wild sound, as if a wolf had risen out of his heart. "You will speak of this no more!" He flung my hand from his arm and turned away, refusing to see my silent tears.

Chapter 12

Because I had embarrassed myself with Father Colin, I couldn't bear to see him, so I stayed away from the church and my favorite little chapel dedicated to the Virgin. I tried to pray in my room or in the quiet of the garden below my window, but even that was difficult.

The only way I could find any solace was to go back to the places where I knew I could find Benno and Pippa and the others, although I now made it a practice to go only when I knew Father Colin would most likely be saying his obligatory prayers in his room or in the church. The little group, which was growing daily, had become my family and the only place I could find happiness. I had become particularly fond of Balbina because, in spite of their differences, she still reminded me somehow of Teresa.

"Is it a grand house you live in?" she asked me, sounding like Teresa. "As grand as a castle?"

Instead of filling Balbina's head with gossamer dreams as I had when I answered Teresa by telling her that one day she would come to live with me in the grand house, I told her the truth.

"Some would call the house I live in a castle, Balbina, but it is not nearly as grand as the house I lived in as a peasant, although some might call that a hovel."

"You talk in circles without making sense," Balbina said.

"I'm not as happy where I live now," I said. "It takes more than size and rich furnishings to make a house grand."

To Balbina any house would be grand, and I ached to find a way to help her have one. It sickened me to think that she would end up living as Fausta lived, if she was lucky enough to survive enough winters to be of an age for such a loathsome fate.

I had not seen Fausta again, but that was because to reach the district where she lived, I would have to pass near the church and risk seeing Father Colin. Perhaps it was foolish pride that kept me away.

The comfort I found in visiting those I'd come to think of as my family wasn't enough to lift my spirits entirely. My dark mood became obvious to the household. If I could have gone down to the kitchen for a chat with Rufina and Grimani I might have felt better, even if I could never tell them, or anyone, the reason for my gloom. Yet I stayed away from the kitchen. Concetta kept too close a watch on me, and the fear of Dominico beating me again for displeasing him hung over me and only added weight to my heavy feelings.

Concetta's reaction to my dark mood was to become more suspicious of me and to keep a closer watch on me. I wasn't aware that Dominico had sensed my state of mind until the third night, when I was summoned to dine with him and Lorenzia.

"Your sour spirit is tiresome, woman," he said. Obviously he had no concern for me or for what might be causing the darkness, and for that I could be grateful.

"She cares not that a woman with child must guard against dark humor." Lorenzia spoke with an air of satisfaction as well as authority.

I ignored her and glanced at Dominico and tried to smile. Certainly it wouldn't do for him to question me about my mood, so I would pretend to banish it. "I'm sorry, sir. I didn't mean to appear either sour or tiresome."

"See that you work harder at it," he said, stuffing his mouth full of roasted pigeon. "We dine tomorrow with Melozzo and his wife. Everyone will be there. I don't want you embarrassing me."

"Rest assured that I will not, sir." I hoped that my smile didn't appear as forced as it felt.

That night he came to me in my room and lay with me, and once again he failed at his attempt at coupling. At least he was content afterward to let it go with a string of vile curses before he fell asleep next to me. I slept little because of his snores.

During the night a wind arrived, roaring and screaming. I could hear it winding itself around and through the thick, bare branches of the trees in the garden below, and I could feel its cold, wet tongue flicking through the closed shutters of the bedroom. I shivered and curled myself into a ball, but I refused to roll closer to Dominico to take in his warmth, as I used to with Teresa.

Dawn arrived, the color of ash, and I rose from the bed to breakfast with Dominico in the cold room. It had become his habit to have our breakfast brought to us after a night together. His purpose was so that Concetta would see that we had been together. It was all a part of his elaborate ruse to convince others of his virility. I'm certain he knew, as I did, that she would gossip freely with servants from other houses, who, in turn, would spread any delicious tidbits—greatly exaggerated, of course—to their masters.

"Will you be going out again this morning, signora?" Concetta asked as she made an elaborate show of placing our bowls of hot porridge and plates of bread in exact balance to one another.

"No." I purposely kept my answer to no more than that one word with the hope that it would discourage her from pressing the matter further. I didn't want to have to justify or explain anything to Dominico about my regular ventures out of the house.

"Ah, then you won't be meeting the young priest. I only wanted to know if I should help you dress for the wind and cold." Her words sounded as bland as mush, but there was a vile pus in them meant to infect me as well as Dominico.

"I am meeting no one," I said, hoping to end it there.

She dropped her head and clasped her hands in front of her in the most humble of poses. "Forgive me, signora. I must have seemed impertinent with my remark. I've seen you walking with the priest to and from the church along the market street. I had no right to assume you met regularly."

By this time my face felt flushed and my heart pounded a heavy rhythm, but I said nothing, since everything I'd said to this point had only made matters worse. Dominico was silent as well, except to ask Concetta to bring scissors so he could trim his beard. We ate our breakfast in silence, save the sound of the wind, and it was not until Concetta brought the scissors and left the room again that Dominico finally spoke.

"What have you been doing with the young priest?"

"I am mindful that you have forbidden me to speak to him, sir, but I cannot stop his speaking to me." I returned the morsel of bread I'd just picked up to the plate again so Dominico wouldn't see that my hand was trembling.

"Why do you meet him on Market Street?"

"He passes the intersection of Church Street and Market Street when he goes to help the poor. I pass the same intersection when I go to the church to pray." I pretended to be busy brushing crumbs from my nightdress as I spoke.

Dominico pushed his breakfast tray back and stood up from the table. I could feel his hard, cruel gaze as he looked down at me. "He passes the intersection regularly?"

"Somewhat regularly, I think. I've seen him a few times." I kept my head down, refusing to meet his gaze.

"You will change your hour of prayer."

"I have already done that, sir." That, at least, was not a lie. I really was making an effort to avoid Father Colin.

Dominico mumbled something incomprehensible and walked toward the door. He turned back just as he opened it. "See that you look your best tonight."

"Yes, sir," I said, still without looking at him. When I heard the door close behind him, I fell to my knees and begged for forgiveness for my sins of lust and falsehood. It is true that the words I spoke to my husband were not lies, but I had twisted them with the devil's cunning so that his understanding of them would be false. I asked Saint Mary of Magdala to intercede for me for forgiveness of my sins, and I asked the Holy Mother to guide me in making me pure and more worthy. Tears streamed down my face out of sorrow for my sins as well as from the tension and fear Dominico raised in me.

I was still on my knees when I heard the soft knock at the door and was in the process of trying to stand and, at the same time, wipe the tears from my face when Concetta opened the door. She always knocked as she was required to do, but she never waited to be admitted. Rather, she simply barged in immediately. That habit both annoyed me and made me feel uncomfortable, but I was not trained in the ways a lady spoke to her servants, so I didn't know how to ask her to mend her ways.

"Forgive me, my lady. I see that I've interrupted your prayers." As usual, she was careful in the way she framed her remarks, but I could hear the mocking in her voice and sense the satisfaction I imagined she felt for having told Dominico about my past rendezvous with Father Colin. "I've come to help you dress," she said, tugging at my nightdress.

"I'll dress myself. Leave me, please." I did my best to sound neither contrite nor upset. I didn't want to give her the satisfaction of knowing that her poison had hit its mark and made Dominico suspicious.

"If you go to meet the priest you will need an underdress, because the weather is unusually cold today."

A sudden flame of anger flared inside me. "I will decide for myself when I need an underdress, and I told you I am meeting no one. Nevertheless, if I should decide to meet the priest or the bishop, or indeed, the pope himself, it is of no concern to you." Even I was surprised at the harshness in my voice.

Concetta blanched and took a backward step. "Of course, signora. Forgive me, signora." She bowed and left the room. In spite of her contrite gesture, there was something about her— the way her upper lip stretched across her yellow teeth and the cold look in her eyes—that made me worry. I pushed it out of my mind, though, and went about dressing myself.

I screwed up my courage enough to leave the house by way of the kitchen so I could ask Rufina for a pot of the hot porridge we had had for breakfast. Rufina fussed at me. "You've no business out in this weather. Mind you stay out of sight, you hear?" But she poured the porridge for me. As usual, I wore the ragged dress under my cloak when I left the house, then removed my shoes just before I reached the gathering place of the poor near the market square. I kept my cloak this time. The wind clawed at me with its cold fingers and flung ice needles as well.

There was a small fire burning, and, as usual, a group of people huddled around it. I hurried toward them with the porridge. Before I reached them I heard someone crying out, "She comes! She comes! God's angel has come to us." The words embarrassed me, but I tried to ignore them and to think only of serving the food. I set the pot down and dipped out a ladleful to hand to the woman nearest me.

"Take a little and pass it around. See that each person has some. If there's not enough, I'll try to bring . . ." My words trailed off, and I felt my heart lurch when I saw Father Colin approaching with a load of wood in his arms. He saw me at the same time and hesitated a moment before he walked forward again.

"Good morning, signora. 'Tis not a day for a lady to be walking about with no shoes," he said in his funny accent. He spoke as if nothing had passed between us.

My only response was to greet him with a nod. I did not wish to have to lie to Dominico again about speaking to the priest. I went back to dipping out porridge and passing the ladle around.

"Give me a portion for Pippa." I looked up to see that it was Benno who had spoken. He was pushing his way through the small crowd, and as soon as my eyes locked with his, he added, "Go to her, Margherita. She's not well."

The look on his face frightened me. I filled the ladle and stepped toward Benno. At the same time I saw him glance at Father Colin and give him a slight nod. I was afraid of what that nod meant—that she was in need of him to bless her and forgive her sins before it was too late. Pippa was a short distance away, bundled in a thin, worn coat and lying on the ground with a ragged old boot folded under her head for a pillow. She flailed about, turning first to one side and then the other, and stopped only when a coughing spell left her too weak to turn. I tried to give her some of the porridge, but she pushed it away. She shivered with cold, so I took my cloak from my shoulders and spread it over her, tucking it around her body, fighting against the wind to make it stay in place. Her body felt hot.

"Pippa . . ."

"Little saint? Is that you?" Something rattled deep in her chest, and it seemed hard for her to breathe. The wind, blowing across her face, robbed even more of her breath.

"It's me, Margherita," I said.

"And Father?" she asked, reaching a hand toward Father Colin. He took her hand and folded her fingers around a rosary and began to pray in a low voice.

"How long have you been like this?" I whispered, not wanting to disturb the priest's prayers.

"Only a few days," Pippa said. She gasped for breath and clawed at the air as if she might grasp it and bring it to her lungs.

I brought my face close to hers so she could hear me above the wind. "I'll bring you a poultice. The cook is skillful at making them. Just wait, and I'll—"

"No," she said, reaching for my hand as if to keep me beside her. "I want you to be here when . . ." I heard the ghastly rattle in her chest again, and her eyes rolled back until only the whites showed.

I screamed her name, and for a second she seemed to look at me before her eyes turned white again. Father Colin glanced at me, shaking his head while he continued his blessing and prayers. I dropped my head to her chest and lay against her, praying silently. I stopped, full of fear and dread, when I heard the rattling cease. Father Colin made the sign of the cross, then bent to whisper a final blessing in her ear before he closed the lids over her colorless eyes.

"Pippa. Oh, Pippa."

"She's at peace now," Father Colin said. He took my cloak from her body, then stood and held it for me.

"No!" I said, and pulled the cloak over Pippa, tucking it around her body again. "She's still warm," I said. "I don't want her to get . . ." Sobs tumbled from my throat, making it impossible to talk.

"She won't get cold now," Father Colin said, taking my arm in a gentle gesture and leading me away. "She will be warm forever and never hungry. She will have beautiful white raiments and a crown of gold."

His words reminded me of the fantastic descriptions I had woven in the past to comfort Teresa, sometimes knowing they weren't true, but I let him talk and let him lead me a short distance away and let him hold me, his body shielding me from the wind. In a little while I pulled away from him.

"Forgive me," I said, swiping at my eyes with the backs of my hands. "I embarrass you, I know. I'll go now, and I'll take comfort in knowing Pippa's sins are forgiven and that your prayers are so powerful that she will soon be in heaven."

"Margherita!" he said, grabbing my arm as I moved away. "I must tell you"—he hesitated, looking into my eyes—"that I am leaving."

I couldn't speak. I could only look at him, trying to take in what he had said.

"I can't stay here. You know that. I will go to the monastery of San Pietro in Vale, where I can pray and meditate and live the life I have vowed to live."

I wanted to tell him that I didn't want him to go, that I was truly sorry I had caused him this pain, but I could say none of that. All I could do was shake my head. He held my face with both his hands and looked into my eyes.

"You don't embarrass me, Margherita. Your goodness

193

leaves me in awe. You make me happy. You make me glad to be alive. You make me love you in a way that I must not love you."

"Colin," I said. It was the first time I had spoken his name without his priestly title. There was a strange force whirling around us, drawing us together as we stood looking into each other's eyes, his hands still on my face. In the next moment his lips were on mine, and I felt as if the angels surrounded us, as if I'd never been kissed until that moment. In all too short a time he pulled away, looked at me one last time, and turned his back to walk away. He stopped when he reached Pippa's body and picked her up, carrying her as he might carry a child. I watched him until he disappeared into the gray of the morning.

Chapter 13

SORROW AND LONGING for him made my soul heavy and my thoughts unfocused as I made my way back to the house. I had left my cloak wrapped around Pippa, and when I stopped to retrieve my shoes from their hiding place, they weren't there. Whoever had taken them would undoubtedly need them more than I did, I thought, and continued my walk home. I scarcely felt the cold or the lack of cloak or shoes. The pain I felt at losing Colin, as well as Pippa's death, overwhelmed all of it.

I hardly remembered the walk home or even entering the house, but I at least had enough of my senses about me to change into a proper dress and shoes and to hide the old rag I wore before Concetta came to my room to help me dress for the evening out with Dominico. The self-satisfied attitude she'd assumed earlier that morning when she had managed to make Dominico suspicious and angry was still with her. Whatever her mood, it no longer mattered to me now. I was certain I would never see Colin again, so she would have no reason to plant suspicion in Dominico's mind.

She was less talkative tonight, and for that I was grateful. The only reason I had to speak to her was to answer her about which dress I wished to wear, whether I wanted my hair wound or plaited, and whether or not I wished to cover it with a cap. I'm not certain I could have controlled my emotions if I'd had to do more than that.

When at last she left my room, I did my best to pray. I asked both of my saints to forgive me for loving Colin, to help me lose my awful sadness, and to somehow get me through the evening that lay ahead. Although I prayed with as much sincerity and piety as I could muster, I had a hollow feeling. My words were sounds without meaning, and I felt as if there were no one listening anyway. I had just risen from my impotent prayers when the knock came at the door and Concetta told me Dominico had sent for me.

At least he wasn't in a sullen mood. Instead he seemed preoccupied with something—the French market, I supposed. Whatever it was, he was distracted and spoke to me very little, except to caution me again that I was to conduct myself properly and not embarrass him. He always gave me the same caution, in spite of the fact that, except for that first time at the Urbinos' house when I lost my dinner in front of everyone, I had never embarrassed him again. I learned it was best to do little more than sit quietly and smile at these banquets we attended. I did the same at the occasional one he hosted at his house. I spoke only when good manners required it, and then as politely and briefly as possible. I had gained the reputation of being shy and perhaps a little dull or even slow-witted, which suited me fine. Apparently it satisfied Dominico as well, since he never railed at me for misbehavior after or during one of these social events. He was content to bask in his pride of my growing belly and take all of the credit for it. The little deception was beneficial to both of us, so we never mentioned it.

Grateful for his near silence as we made our way to the house of Melozzo, I walked in silence as well. I wasn't certain I could hide my feelings if I were forced to talk. In spite of the cocoon of despair that held me, I at least had enough of my wits about me to recognize that snow was falling and sticking to our path. It gave me hope that it would provide a reason for Dominico to want to leave the party early.

A merry scene greeted us when Signora Melozzo opened the door to us. We were met with a rush of warm air, and inside her house a large red fire danced in the fireplace. Men and women stood or lounged around the room, sipping on what appeared to be cups of laughter. In spite of the gaiety that was always a part of these gatherings, I never felt comfortable. I wasn't interested in the gossip about sexual liaisons and misconduct that seemed so amusing to everyone else. I scarcely understood the talk of local politics, and the fact that the pope resided in Avignon instead of Rome was of no concern to me, since both cities were equally foreign to me.

The faces of wives and daughters among this group had become familiar, as had their names, yet I couldn't say I knew them. When they gathered in little clusters to laugh and talk, I always felt left out. It was no different this time. The beautiful woman, Signora Melozzo, who had flirted so much with Dominico the first time I accompanied him to a social gathering, did at least speak to me.

"So there you are, Margherita," she said in her throaty voice that always seemed on the verge of laughter. "I was afraid you wouldn't join us tonight."

"Oh, come now, Grazia," the plump woman called Clarise said. "She's no more than four or five months gone on her pregnancy. Not enough to keep her home abed yet."

"No, no, it wasn't her pregnancy but her piety that I thought would keep her away." Grazia never took her eyes off of me.

Rather than speaking to me, they spoke about me, as if I weren't there. That made me uncomfortable, but not nearly as uncomfortable as the reference to my piety. Was there gossip about my frequent meetings with Colin? Had I really been so careless?

"Piety?" Clarise said with a laugh. "Dominico would never stand for a wife who was overly pious. And besides, what pious saint would find herself in the condition she's in so early in the marriage?"

"Ah, then, perhaps she was only being penitent," Grazia said, leveling the smile that matched her name on me. "Is that what you were doing?"

"I . . . I don't understand." I kept my head down, and my words were pitifully stammering.

"Walking alone in the snow? Wearing rags and no shoes? I must say you would be the envy of the most pious mendicant."

There was another laugh from Clarise. "Grazia, are you making jokes? I've never before seen your cruel side."

"Cruel?" Grazia said, turning away from me to face her. "I'm curious rather than cruel. I saw her with my own eyes, barefoot and in rags as it snowed." She turned back to me. "Tell me," she said, whispering conspiratorially, "are you really so pious? Were you doing penance for your sins?"

I felt trapped and forced to say something. "I . . . I'm not nearly as pious as I might wish." I managed to raise my eyes a little to look at her. "It's only that . . . that I wish to give succor to the poor, and they find me more . . . more acceptable if I humble myself." I hated myself for stammering, but more than anything I was frightened. I had been careless today by walking home without my cloak and shoes and had allowed myself to be seen. Had Dominico seen me as well? And if he hadn't seen me, wouldn't the gossip soon reach his ears?

That fear, coupled with the still-heavy sadness I felt for the loss of Colin, served to distract me to the point that I was unaware that we had been summoned to table until everyone was there except me. I made my way alone and embarrassed and sat in the only vacant chair. My odd behavior didn't go unnoticed, and I felt several curious eyes on me as I sat down. At least Dominico, who was seated several chairs down from me and on the opposite side of the table, didn't appear to notice. He was deep in conversation with a man and woman seated to his left. For that I was grateful.

After the meal was served and the endless toasts had begun, Dominico rose from his chair and left the room. That gave me no reason for worry, since, with all the wine that was drunk at such gatherings, both men and women often left the table to relieve themselves outdoors or, sometimes in the case of ladies, to borrow a chamber pot. My lack of concern soon gave way to bewilderment. I suddenly realized he had left without me.

My confusion sprang from the thought that he would be embarrassed when others learned we didn't leave together. Relief for having an excuse to leave, however, was my primary emotion. As quickly as I could, I retrieved my cloak and slipped out the door. White petals of snow drifted from the sky in a hurry to cover the town, including the path home. Any footprints Dominico might have left were obscured by now. I made my way up the street toward his house in the odd hush of a snow-bright night with my cloak tucked around me and my head down collecting tiny wet drifts in the folds of my cap, and willing my mind to be as numb as my limbs.

I hardly looked up at all until I walked through the gate and started up the walkway to the house. That was when I saw Dominico. He was partially covered with snow as he waited at the top of the entrance steps, arms folded, and looking like a great white stone statue.

I stopped and looked up at him. "Dominico? Are you ill?"

"No," he said, never taking his eyes off of me.

I continued walking toward him until I had climbed the steps and stood in front of him. "Because you left early without me, I thought perhaps your headache had—"

He grabbed me suddenly, twisting my arm behind me with such force I thought the limb might leave its socket. I cried out, and he struck me across my mouth. Blood warmed my face, and I felt momentarily stunned.

"Is it not enough that you disobey me?" he said in the voice of a beast I didn't recognize. "Must you embarrass me with your insane piety as well?"

I tried to speak, to tell him that I had never meant to embarrass him, but before I could form the words he hit me again. This time his knuckles struck the socket of my eye, and a white-hot pain migrated from beneath my eye to my ear and throat and neck.

"You wear rags? You walk the winter streets barefooted like the vermin who live around the market square? Why? What's your excuse, wife?" He twisted my arm even harder, as if he would force an answer from me.

"The poor," I said, barely managing to choke out the words. "If I am to help them, I must become as one of them. I—"

"Your damned piety. Who told you to do that? The priest? What else does he have you do? Warm his bed, of course."

I shook my head. "No! Never! You must never think that I—"

"Don't tell me what to think, woman. I'll teach you obedience. I'll teach you not to embarrass me."

With that he struck me again, with such force that my body turned, and I felt my feet slip on the snow-slick steps. I fell forward, hitting the first step so hard I thought my belly would burst. I cried out in a pitiful voice, "My baby!" And in the next moment I felt the hard toe of Dominico's boot in my stomach, then in my side as I rolled over to protect my child, and then, finally, low in my back. The final blow made me roll and bounce down the remaining steps, and all the while I was trying to protect my womb with my arms.

I heard Dominico's angry voice again, shouting that he would not be embarrassed. For an instant I saw his distorted face, teeth bared, lips thin, and eyes spewing rage. At the same time I felt as if something had gripped my womb and twisted it, and I felt a warm, sticky gush between my legs. I watched it leave my body.

A bright red river in the white, white snow.

Someone screamed, crying out for her child and for the Holy Mother and Saint Mary of Magdala to protect her. Was it my own cry? I wasn't sure. It was as if I stood outside my body, looking down at the crumpled woman and at the bloody mess that oozed from her body. It occurred to me that, in spite of her plea to the saints, I was the only one who heard.

I have no memory of anything more until I awakened in a bed that at first seemed strange to me. I felt a dull ache all around my middle and in my head. I lay on my side with my knees pulled up to my chest, and my entire body was damp with sweat. Someone hovered over me, someone with blurred features and a muffled voice. I cried out and rolled over, trying to sit up, trying to escape the creature who, I was certain, would strike me again.

"It's all right. It's all right," the voice said, clearer this time. I felt hands forcing me down. Gentle hands. A voice I recognized.

"Rufina?"

"Hush, child."

My vision cleared enough that I recognized her face as well. I sat up quickly, pushing away her gentle hands. "Rufina! What are you doing in here? If Dominico sees you he'll surely beat both of us. Go! Go!" My sudden movement left me feeling dizzy, and the room darkened.

I tried to force her away, but she captured my hands and made me lie down again, all the while murmuring, "Hush, child, hush. It's all right. It's all right."

All I could do was lie still and look at her with my eyes wide while I tried to focus. I was too weak to do anything else. As I stared at her, I tried to make sense of what was happening. Then memory pierced my consciousness like a sharp knife— Dominico pushing me, the fall down the steps, the cramping pain, the bloody issue. Along with those memories came a horrible snake of a sound rising from my throat, writhing and twisting throughout the room like something not of this earth, something terrible and haunted.

"Margherita, Margherita." Rufina's voice was a plea for me to be comforted, but I would not be. I knew what had happened to me. On rare occasions I'd seen it before—the blood, the half-formed creature dropping from a she-animal who was sick or who had been wounded.

My keening continued—one long word of sorrow without a breath until the sound was all out of me. Finally I lay limp and exhausted.

Rufina sat on the bed and picked up my hand and spoke to me. "Rest. That's all you can do now and all you must do." She spoke in a soft, quiet voice I'd never heard her use before. "Here, drink this," she said, and held a cup to my lips. It had a bitter taste, and I tried to refuse it, but she forced me to drink it anyway.

With the bitter taste still lingering on my tongue, I put my free hand on my flat stomach. "Gone," I said.

"Gone," she whispered in reply.

My eyes went to the door, where I expected Dominico to enter any moment. "You must leave."

"No," she said. "Have no fear. The beast Vasari bade me come to you."

I gave her a questioning look.

"He was afraid when he saw you and all the blood, and he called for Grimani to bring you inside. No, no, hush now," she said, holding my shoulders back when I tried to sit up again. "Grimani brought you here, and Vasari sent for Signora Lorenzia and Concetta, but you wouldn't stop screaming. You called for me. Over and over again you called for me. Grimani told me you were like a wild animal. Neither the signora nor Concetta could do anything with you. You kept screaming until finally Vasari gave in and sent for me. Grimani wouldn't leave you with him. He made Concetta come for me." Rufina laughed, a sharp little sound. "You should have seen her face. It had gone white—more from anger at having to come for me than fear for you, I would say. You fell, she said. Slipped on the ice. The same story Vasari told, but I could see the truth in Grimani's eyes. And in Vasari's, too, the fool." Rufina shook her head, and tears streaked her face. "I knew when I saw Concetta bring your shoes inside to give to the signora. I knew they would tell him, and I knew what he would do to you."

"Concetta had my shoes? She must have followed me and found them."

"She may have followed you," Rufina said. She closed her eyes and shook her head. "But she would have learned the truth soon enough anyway. There was gossip among some of the servants from other houses, them what has family or friends what lives homeless on the streets and hears things. They're calling you the barefoot angel, or even the barefoot saint." Rufina shook her head. "Whatever the manner that Concetta learned what you were doing, she couldn't wait to see

Vasari and the old signora so she could present them with the truth. I saw her take the shoes to Lorenzia, and she must have shown them to Vasari after he returned without you."

"But he knew even before then," I said in a voice grown hoarse from my keening. "There were others who robbed Concetta of the pleasure of being the first to tell him. The merchants and their wives have seen me as well. I've been careless. And foolish."

Rufina's only reply was to look at me with a troubled expression I couldn't read.

"Why did God take my baby?" My voice was weak and hoarse, but even I could hear the anger in it.

"Wasn't God what took it. Was the devil Vasari." She made no attempt to hide her own anger.

"I cried out to God. I asked for the Holy Mother and for Maria of Magdala to help me. Why did they abandon me?" I wanted to weep, but I had no more tears, and I was beginning to feel very tired.

Rufina shook her head. "Don't ask me such as that. I'm nothing but a poor cook in a rich man's house. I come from the same peasant stock as you. It's not given to us to know. But you'd serve yourself well to keep in mind that the devil's evil is strong and cunning."

"Is the devil stronger and more cunning than God and all the saints?"

"How would a person like me know such things? But

there's some what says you'll burn in hell for asking such as that."

"Will God condemn me for seeking answers to something I don't know?" I turned my head away from her. "Let him condemn me and strike me dead if he will. I care nothing for life anyway."

"Hush! Now's not the time for self-pity."

"It's not self-pity I feel. It's despair. I would curse God and die." I had lost much on this day, I thought. I'd lost my lover and my child, and I had long ago lost my family. What cause did I have to live?

"Why waste your breath? If he hears not your prayers, will he hear your curses?"

I looked at her, silent for a moment while my poor, weary mind tried to sort out her meaning. "Perhaps there is no God," I said.

"If there's not, would you serve him anyway? Or would you let the hungry starve? The naked go without clothes? The thirsty go without water?"

"I . . . I would . . ."

She stood and looked down at me as I lay in bed. "You have risked your life to help them. You have sacrificed your firstborn out of your passion to help them. Out of your love for them. And you say there is no God? I say he lives within your soul."

I don't know what happened after that. She must have left

the room, and I must have fallen asleep. The bitter drink she gave me had done it, perhaps, because I had thought I was too angry and too much in despair to sleep. Did I dream? I wasn't sure. I saw a woman sometime later, sitting next to my bed and wearing the white robes of the Virgin. She spoke to me, but I couldn't hear her words clearly—something about feeding the poor and giving drink to the thirsty. It was the Holy Mother, but she had Rufina's face.

Chapter 14

THERE WERE NO MORE visions after the night I lost my baby. I began to doubt and to wonder if my recent vision had been no more than a dream brought on by Rufina's herbs. I told myself there could be no visions, since neither God nor heaven existed. Or if they did exist, I preferred to shut myself off from them. I wanted nothing to do with a God so cruel.

I stayed in my room for weeks, refusing to go out, eating little or nothing of the food brought to me. If I slept I didn't know it, since it had become impossible for me to know sleep from wakefulness. I suppose Dominico must have become concerned, since he sent Lorenzia to talk to me.

When she knocked on my door, I was in bed with the shutters closed and no candle burning to give the room light. I heard the knock, but I didn't respond. It would have taken more energy than I possessed. I might not have even opened my eyes had not the dim light that seeped in from the hall when she opened the door seemed unbearably blinding. I covered my eyes with my forearm as she entered and spoke my name.

"Margherita!" She waited for my response, and when there

was none she let loose her vile tongue. "There's no need for this nonsense. Do you think you're the only woman who's lost a child? You should have been up and about long ago. Your master is not pleased that you are pretending such hysterics, and neither am I."

Again I didn't respond, not out of disrespect or petulance, but because there seemed to be nothing to say. I wanted no more than to die.

"You should be up now, eager to make another baby. Dominico has been surprisingly patient with you, but no man's patience is everlasting. Arise now and make yourself worthy of him." Again she waited in vain for my response, and when there was none she expelled a disgusted sigh, then left, slamming the door.

Dominico didn't come to my room himself, but he did send Rufina again. I was up sitting in a chair and staring down at the little garden when I heard her knock and her voice asking for permission to enter. I turned my head toward the door.

"Rufina?" I hadn't spoken in so long, just saying her name made my throat ache.

She opened the door and stuck her head inside in a cautious gesture before she entered and walked to my side.

"Vasari bade me come, but I would have come long ago on my own had he allowed it."

I wanted to reach my hand to hold hers to show my appreciation, but I had not the strength. All I seemed to know to do was return to staring out the window. It was she who took my hand after she knelt beside my chair. "You have reason to grieve, as we all know, but I beg of you, don't give him the pleasure of knowing you grieved yourself unto death."

It made no difference to me whether my death gave him pleasure or not, so I saw no need to respond.

"You're too thin, child. You must eat more. I'll make honey cakes for you."

I tried to shake my head and tell her I had no desire for food, but I wasn't able to speak. All I could manage was to turn my face away from the window and look at her. That seemed to cheer her some. She smiled, patted my hand, and left. Since I had lost all accounting of time, I'm not certain how long it was before the honey cakes showed up on the tray that Concetta regularly brought to my room, but I suspect it couldn't have been long.

Although I secretly resented Rufina's constantly referring to me as "child," I was, in truth, still little more than one. I couldn't resist a tiny nibble at the sweet cake. It was enough to encourage her, because the cakes began to show up on my tray regularly. After the first bite I seldom tasted them, though. I preferred to subsist solely on water and a bit of bread. In time I allowed Concetta to help me dress, but my clothes hung on me like the loose flesh of an old horse, and my arms and elbows looked like pigeon bones on a fat man's plate.

Eventually I was summoned to dine with my husband.

Once dressed, I made my way downstairs and sat at table once again with Dominico and Lorenzia. There was much bickering and arguing between them, although I was unable, or unwilling, to comprehend the meaning of any of it. I'm certain there was also an equal amount of anger expressed toward me, which I ignored, except to note in the slightest way a growing understanding of the power my lack of response gave me.

By the time spring arrived I had taken to sitting regularly in the garden, which I could now enter or leave whenever I pleased. I still had not left the house. I even refused to go to church, although Dominico demanded it, and threatened harm to me if I did not. It was important to him, I knew, for us to be seen there. As he said, it was good for business. But what did I care about business? Or what did I care if he beat me? My mute placidness had finally robbed him of his power. He sensed my disinterest, and I was spared his punishment.

I came to understand, by way of Rufina's chatter, that Dominico was spreading the story that my miscarriage as well as my fall on the icy steps had seriously endangered my health, and that I had been advised by the local physician to stay abed most of the time.

The truth was, I had never seen a physician. "Just as well you never see him," Rufina once told me. "He's killed far more than he's healed."

Rufina had easy access to me now, and I to her. The fact that she often came to my room to bring food or simply to see to my well-being angered Concetta, and she threatened to leave. Rufina took great joy in telling me that Dominico told her to leave when she wished, as he would provide no references and she would find herself begging for her food or selling her body.

"Ah, her fortunes have turned," Rufina said one day when I was sitting in the kitchen with her and Grimani. "She thought siding with Lorenzia to cause you trouble with Vasari would make both the signora and the master favor her. Truth is, Vasari is beside himself and favors no one since he's lost his child and, it seems, his wife, as well. Serves her right, I say." She looked up at me from her work of quartering turnips. "He won't be getting him another babe on you, either, will he? Oh, I know the truth; don't think I don't. Fausta told me about the shriveled worm between his legs." She laughed and went on cutting the turnips.

I was aware of the worried and guarded glances she gave me when I didn't respond. I did nothing to change that, for the truth was, I didn't know what to do about the numb and lifeless existence I led. Perhaps I didn't even realize that anything needed to be done.

It occurred to me that I would have liked to spend my time reading if I'd possessed the skill. A few women I knew did know how to read and how to write poetry as well. There was no one to teach me, save Dominico, but even if he lowered himself to tutor me, I could never bear to be in his presence long enough to learn.

So I sat in the garden or in the kitchen. It was while I was sitting in the kitchen again one afternoon when the days were growing longer, stretching toward summer, that we all heard a knock at the back entrance.

"Now who could that be?" Rufina said, sounding annoyed. "I'm expecting no deliveries or workmen today, and I have not the time for gossip." In spite of what she said, she wiped her hands on the sides of her dress and hurried toward the door, as if she were, in truth, eager for gossip. Grimani, who no longer had to worry about signaling me to hide in the larder when someone approached, merely chuckled as she rushed past him.

When she opened the door, I could see an old candlewick of a woman, slightly stooped and with a grooved, waxy face. "Rufie?" she said with a little cough. "It's me. Don't you recognize me?"

It was then that I noticed the dirty, rumpled dress she wore. A dress that had once been mine.

"Fausta?" I said, standing up from the chair in my silent corner. "Is it really you?" I walked toward her, but I was weak, and my steps were slow.

"Dear God, it is!" Rufina gave a quick and cautious glance over her shoulder. We all knew there would be hell to pay if Dominico or the signora knew Fausta was there. Rufina reached for her to pull her inside, but Fausta jerked away.

"No," she said in her hoarse voice. "If Vasari saw me in his house . . ." She peered around Rufina's solid and sturdy frame.

"I've come to see the young mistress to . . . Ah! There you are, signora," she said. She smiled when she saw me approaching her. That smile revealed a mouth full of vacant slots. *"Santa Madre!"* she said, and her smile disappeared. "You're too thin. Don't you know you should eat twice as much when you suckle a babe?"

I reached my arms toward her, and we fell into each other's embrace there in the doorway. She had the smell of sickness about her, but it mattered little to me now. I hadn't realized how much I'd missed her.

"You stopped coming. I thought you were ill. The people near the market square said you must have died of childbed sickness." Fausta held me at arm's length as if to make certain I was there. "I wanted to come here so many times, but I was afraid at first, and then the winter came and took its toll on me. Would have starved for certain with no work, except that the girls shared their food and nursed me through the worst of the consumption."

"Fausta!" That one word was all I could speak. I spoke so little those days that I had lost my ability to handle conversation with ease. "Consumption?" I finally managed to say. At that same moment I felt ashamed. I had been so absorbed in my own self-pity that I had become selfish and allowed myself to forget that others suffered more than I.

"It's nothing," Fausta said with a wave of her hand. "Look at me; I'm up and about now, so it's nothing. But what of you?

Oh, I'm so glad you're still alive. How I wish I could see the babe! All the girls are wondering about it too. Is it a man child? Or a little girl, pretty as you?"

We were still standing in the doorway with Rufina and Grimani hovering over us. I felt Grimani's hand on my shoulder as if to steady me, and at the edge of my eye I saw him shake his head, signaling Fausta not to ask more. It served only to alarm her.

"What?" That one word made her cough, but her eyes held the question.

"There is no babe," Rufina said, taking her arm and this time forcing her to come inside. "Don't worry; Grimani will keep watch," she said when Fausta resisted again.

"No babe, you say? Oh, no, the poor thing didn't—"

"Hush now. Margherita will tell you the story when she's ready," Rufina said.

Fausta turned her haunted eyes on me again, and I tried to speak. "Dominico . . ." I felt suddenly very tired, and it was too much of an effort to say more. Instead I looked at Rufina and then at Grimani. They interpreted my look immediately and launched into the story for Fausta, first one relating it and then the other, with Rufina, of course, taking the lead. Fausta interrupted occasionally with cursing and vile names for Dominico.

"And the poor child has hardly spoken a word or eaten a morsel since," Rufina said, finishing the story. "Look at her, how poor of flesh she is, and her spirit's gone."

Fausta stared at me with sadness in her eyes. "It's a woman's lot to suffer," she said, "and a pox on him what made it that way."

Rufina crossed herself in a quick, jerky gesture. "Fausta, you would curse the Creator?"

"Never said it was the Creator. Never said I knew who made things that way. But maybe you're right. Don't I remember the priest saying God put a curse on Eve that all women would suffer?"

"Enough!" Rufina said. At the same time Grimani struck his heavy knife against the pot that hung above his butcher block. Acting with a swiftness I thought I was no longer capable of, I grabbed Fausta's arm and pulled her, not into the larder where there would not be enough room for the two of us, but to the door and out into the alley.

Once we were outdoors, Fausta laughed. "Ah, so you've worked out signals, I see," she said between coughs.

"Fausta, you're not well."

She shrugged. "It was given to the likes of me to have a hard life of work and sorrow and die in my prime."

"But the bathhouse," I said, struggling to form the words. "I thought if you went there . . ."

Fausta looked down at the ground and turned her face away from me. "Me? Working the bathhouses?" She gave a little snort of a laugh. "It would take more than your pretty dress to get me accepted there, I'm afraid." She looked up at me again, this time with even more sadness in her eyes. "It was too late for me—me with the consumption and the pink flesh gone from my bones. Gentlemen, like them at the bathhouses, scorn me and turn away looking for the young ones, pretty and plump, the way I once was. And it's no particular comfort to me, knowing the pretty ones will be in my place before their prime."

"But how do you . . . how do you live? Eat?"

"Oh, don't worry about me," she said with a flip of her hand. "There's plenty that don't carry the title of gentleman that yearns for a woman's body. There's plenty that settles for what they can get for a *quattrini* or two."

"I . . . I stopped coming. I am ashamed for . . ."

"Oh, now, don't you go on talking like that, Signora Margherita. You know what old Soft Worm did to you before for trying to help the likes of me. So don't think of such foolishness."

"But you—"

"Shhh," she said, moving a step closer to me and looking over her shoulder and all around us. "I'd best be going, but before I do, I've something to give you."

"To give me?"

"Yes." She looked around again before she pulled something from the bodice of the once elegant dress I'd given her. It was a rolled vellum, such as the kind Dominico sometimes received messages on, and it was sealed properly with stamped wax. She thrust it into my hands, and I took it reluctantly.

218

"You must be mistaken," I said. "I know not how to read."

"Father Colin," she whispered. "He sent it by way of a man who said he'd traveled from the monastery where he'd stopped for a day or two of rest. Father told him to find me. He knew I would deliver it to you. I'd have come sooner had I been able."

"Colin?" I said. "He . . . sent? To me?"

"I must go now," Fausta said, ignoring my bumbling words. "I'll come again when I can." With that she was gone, her gaunt, spindle-shanked body disappearing in a warren of shadows behind the fine houses of merchants.

I stood alone in the alley behind Dominico's house a few moments longer, holding the rolled letter close to my heart for several seconds before I went inside, concealing the precious gift in the folds of my skirt.

The sight of Concetta in the kitchen giving instructions for Dominico's dinner startled me. I shouldn't have been surprised, since I knew someone had prompted the signal from Grimani earlier. It was my guilt at holding the letter from Colin that made me uneasy. Concetta was equally surprised to see me, or at least to see me coming in from the outside. She, like everyone else in the house, had grown used to my sitting silent in my room or in the garden or kitchen. I could only hope it wasn't the kind of surprise that would raise suspicion.

"Where has she been?" she asked, speaking to Rufina. A servant wouldn't dare direct such a question of the mistress of the house, and while I knew she would pay little heed to such a rule if she had been alone with me, she wouldn't risk Rufina or Grimani reporting her insolence to Dominico.

"I'm not in the habit of asking Signora Vasari for an accounting of her whereabouts." Rufina sounded indignant. "And it's none of my business if she hankers for a breath of fresh air." Clever Rufina. She had managed to give Concetta a plausible answer while at the same time putting her in her place.

Concetta's response was an annoyed, "Hmmpf," before she went back to giving Rufina and Grimani their instructions. I took the opportunity to slip out of the kitchen and up to my room. Since Concetta was in the kitchen and Dominico was seeing to his business and Lorenzia never came to my room unless she was ordered to by Dominico, I knew I would have a few moments with no one coming through the door.

Once inside my room I locked the door, knowing it would not stop any of the three intruders I most dreaded, but I hoped it would at least slow any one of them down enough that I would not be caught doing what I was about to do.

Sitting on the edge of my bed, I opened the scroll and smoothed it out with my hands. The ink-dark marks on the vellum bent this way and that and curled around one another, interlocking here, separating there, all of them creating a secret dance that I could not possibly join or understand. All I knew was that Colin had composed this mystery for me, and for that reason it was dear to me.

It could be a testament of his love for me. Perhaps the words were written in rhyme, as love songs were written. Could it be that he was asking me to come to him? Or telling me that he would come for me? It may have been that he was telling me that, while his vows and my marriage kept us apart, his love for me would live forever. My mind played with the strange markings, creating so many beautiful words that I could almost believe I was actually reading them.

I looked at the manuscript dozens of times over the next several days. Sometimes the marks frightened me, and I imagined that they could mean Colin was angry with me and telling me never to think of him again because he loved the Church far more than he could ever love a woman. At other times I worried that the words told a story of an illness or infirmity that had befallen him, and that he was telling me he would be dead by the time the letter reached my hands.

Most of the time I forbade the markings to mean such unhappy things and thought only of words of love. I longed to find someone to read the letter to me, but whom could I ask? Certainly not Dominico or any of his fellow merchants, all of whom could read and cipher at least a little. Certainly not the old priest Venantious or the bishop on the occasions that he visited San Severino. There was no one else I knew who could read, so I kept the letter and its hidden contents to myself.

Knowing that he considered me important enough to trouble himself to write to me gave me new life. I took to spending more time in the garden and in the kitchen, and to talking regularly with Grimani and Rufina. That prompted Grimani to tease me.

"How you talk, little signora! The blessed silence of this kitchen is gone forever. A man doesn't miss the quiet until it is chased away with girlish giggles."

Rufina scolded him and told him to be grateful my soul was mending. In truth, he didn't need the scolding, because each time he teased me, he threw his head back and spewed out delighted laughter. Neither of them guessed that it was a scrawl of words I could not read that had started my mending.

Finally the day came when I knew I had to resume my work. I had wallowed in my sorrow long enough, and I had begun to see, belatedly perhaps, that it had been nothing compared to the eternal suffering of others.

I retrieved my ragged dress from its hiding place and put it on, surprised at how loosely it hung on me. Summer had slithered its way into the world while I sat mute in my sadness, and the season took me by surprise when I realized that I no longer needed a cloak and would therefore have nothing to hide my truth. But why hide it? It had long ago been discovered, and I had paid the price of discovery. I left the house that day in my ragged dress and without my shoes. I carried a basket of food on my arm and the last vestiges of my youth and naïveté in my heart.

Chapter 15

THE DAY I returned to them, not one of them saw me at first. They were busy trying to survive—some of them begging outside the gates, some of them looking for bits of food dropped by vendors and customers in the market square, some of them simply sitting on the ground in what I knew to be a state of despair. They had stopped looking for me the same way I had stopped looking for God and my saints.

I approached a group of three of them, two women and a man. One of the women was rocking back and forth staring straight ahead at nothing until I came into her view carrying my basket, covered with a cloth, on my arm. As soon as I was close enough she spit at me.

"Go away, woman! There's enough misery here without the likes of you."

At first I was surprised at her vehement cry, until I realized she saw me as competition for whatever meager means she had for survival. She certainly expected nothing good from me.

"No need to fear me," I said, walking closer. "I bring—"

Before I could finish the sentence or uncover the basket of food, she threw a rock at me. It struck in the middle of my forehead, and I staggered backward, barely saving myself from falling. The woman huddled next to her picked up another rock and threw it, hitting my arm. By this time blood from my head wound was trickling into my eyes.

"Stop! Stop it, fools!" the man who was with the two women said. He was staggering to his feet, looking groggy, as if he'd just awakened from sleep. I recognized him as a man named Girolamo, one of the group I'd gotten to know earlier. "That's Margherita!" He was struggling with the women, trying to take the rocks from their hands. "She's a saint, you fools. Leave her be!"

"A saint, you say?" the first woman said. "You're the fool, old man. She's a beggar, just like the rest of . . ."

By this time I had managed to uncover the basket, revealing the food. Both of the women rushed toward me and snatched the basket from me.

"No need to be greedy!" Girolamo shouted to their backs. "She can make the food multiply until there's enough for all of us."

The women ignored him and kept running. The ruckus attracted a crowd. Many of the people recognized me, and they hurried to embrace me and to wipe the blood from my face. Others fell at my feet, which embarrassed me greatly, and I did my best to pull them up so I could address them properly.

"Margherita! Margherita! We feared you were dead," some of them cried. Some, to my further embarrassment, called me Saint Margherita or even Saint Barefoot.

"Where's the babe?" one of them called. "You must bring the little one to see us." It was such a happy gathering I was reluctant to tell them the sad truth about my lost child, but they pressed me so hard I finally had to admit that I had lost the baby in the fifth month.

None of them was surprised, since, as Lorenzia had said, I was not the first to lose a child before its birthing time. "Ah, but you're young. There's plenty of time for more," many told me. Their words, meant to comfort, bruised my soul the way the stones had bruised my body, because I knew that, because of my husband's infirmity, I would never have another child.

Many of the faces were familiar to me, but Benno's was not among them. "Where is he?" I asked, trying to be heard over the clamor. "Where is Benno?"

"He's gone," Girolamo said. "Gone the way of all flesh."

I felt what little was left of my spirit vanishing, a puff of smoke swallowed by a cruel wind. "How . . . ?" I had once again lost my ability to speak.

Girolamo shrugged at my unphrased question. "Want of food, maybe. Or the cold. Or maybe it was just that he lost his soul."

Lost his soul? I knew how easily that could happen. I was powerless to stop the loss of my own soul, but I could have helped his hunger. I could have brought him protection against the cold. I felt sickened and stunned, and I felt as if his blood were on my own hands. I vowed then to do all I could to alleviate the misery of these people. At just that moment I heard Rufina's voice in my mind, loud and unbidden. *Even if there is no God, would you serve him anyway?*

Yes, I thought, I would do his work. Out of anger if for no other reason, or because God didn't seem capable or willing to do it himself. If he existed at all, he was unspeakably cruel. I don't know how far that anger and bitterness might have taken me had the moment not been changed by a soft, almost angelic voice.

"Margherita? Is that really you?"

I turned toward the sound and saw the thin but smiling face of Balbina. She had grown a little taller over the winter, although her body still had no womanly flesh.

"Balbina!" I cried, rushing toward her. She still reminded me of my little sister, Teresa.

"I heard you were here," she said. "You've been gone too long." The flint in her eyes and a certain hardness around her mouth suggested that it had been longer than I realized, and that the length of time had not been easy for her. At least she wasn't living in the row of houses on the street behind the church. Not yet, anyway.

"Yes," I said. "I've been gone too long, but I'm back now, and I want to hear all about you."

"No, you don't." Those words, the sound of her voice, made my heart cold. Her gaze held mine for a few seconds, and I saw more in that look than words could express. I had failed her, too. Her mother was dead, and Colin and I had both left her and the others. She must despise me as much as I despised the God I was trying not to acknowledge.

"I won't leave you again," I said.

She smiled. At least hope had not been killed in her.

"I heard you tell them about the baby," she said. "I heard you say you fell on the ice."

"Yes," I said. I hadn't mentioned that Dominico pushed me. I saw no point in it. No matter how I came to fall, the result was the same. Dominico's cruelty and the injustice of what had happened would make no difference to them, since, to these people, cruelty and injustice were everywhere.

"The baby is dead. My mama is dead, too. I could be your child. You could be my mama."

Her words surprised me. I hadn't stopped to think how desperate her need was. I owed her nothing less than the truth. "My husband would not allow you to live in his house," I said. My thoughts were going in another direction. I was thinking how wonderful it would be to have her living with me. How much it would alleviate my longing for Teresa and the sadness over the loss of my baby.

"We need not live in his house," Balbina said. "You could live with us. Out here."

I saw, then, something I'd been too selfish to see until that moment—that her longing was as deep as my own. I put my arms around her and brought her close to me. Her body was thin as wire, her back corrugated from want. There was fear in her, along with the longing, so much fear that she was reluctant to turn loose of me. I held her a long moment until she detached herself to take a piece of bread and a hunk of meat from my basket as one of the others walked by with it on her arm. She ran, as it had become second nature for her and others to do when food was in their possession. She carried the bread in one hand, the meat clamped between her teeth, and used her other hand to grab my arm and pull me along with her. As I followed her, I noticed an ugly festering sore on her arm.

We stopped in a spot where the city wall made a little shaded corner. There was an old blanket there I recognized. It was one Colin had given to her a few months earlier, just as the winter began to show its anger. The blanket was dirty now and well-worn, but it and the shady corner were all Balbina had that was home. The wooden huts Colin had built had no doubt been used for firewood during the winter.

Balbina scrambled rodentlike into her niche. While she stuffed her mouth with one hand, she used the other to signal that I was to sit next to her.

"How long has it been since you had something to eat?" I asked.

She shrugged and pushed more of the bread into her mouth with hands that trembled, whether from joy at finding food or weakness from long lack of it, I didn't know. I resolved to wait until she'd had her fill before I spoke to her again. It was she who broke the silence first, however. She leaned back against the wall with a contented sigh and smiled at me with her grease-stained mouth, but winced and cried out when her wounded arm struck the wall. I picked up her arm and kissed it, wishing I could do more.

"If you live with us . . . with me, will you go back to your husband's house from time to time for our food?" she asked, rubbing her arm.

"If I lived with you, so great would be my husband's anger that I would not likely be allowed to go back."

She frowned, and I could see that my statement troubled her. "He would be so wicked?"

"I am his wife. It's his right to have me there, and it's his right to punish me as he sees fit if I displease him."

Balbina made a little indignant puff with her lips. "Then I'll not be any man's wife. Not ever."

It saddened me to think that she would not likely have the opportunity to make that choice. Eventually some man would get a child on her, and she would be fortunate if he stayed around to help her care for it, but she would never have a true marriage, not even a false one such as the one I endured.

"I think your husband must be very wicked," Balbina said, interrupting my musing.

"It's nothing for you to trouble yourself with," I said, hoping to turn her thoughts in another direction.

"You should have married Father Colin."

Again she'd caught me completely by surprise, and I looked at her, unable to speak.

"He loves you," she said.

"Of course. Just as Our Lord taught us to love."

"I am no longer a child, Margherita, and besides, I heard others say they could tell by the way he looked at you. He loves you as a man loves a woman."

"You must never say such things again, Balbina." My voice was scolding and angry.

"Perhaps I would marry after all, if I could marry a man like Father Colin," she said, ignoring me.

"Balbina!"

"Why can't priests marry?"

"Because Our Lord was not married." I knew the answer to that question only because I had asked it once myself, and my mother told me that was the answer a priest had once given her.

"How do you know?"

"The priests teach us those things."

"How do they know?"

I was beginning to see that having a daughter might have its trying moments. "The priests know things because they can read books, and books contain all the knowledge in the world," I said.

"Then I should like to read books."

"And so would I, but there is no one to teach us, Balbina, so we will have to find our knowledge in other ways."

"You could teach me all kinds of things." She picked up my hand and caressed it, keeping her eyes down as if she were afraid to look directly at me, lest I refuse her.

"I would be happy to teach you, Balbina, but I know so very little."

She raised her eyes, daring to look at me as she said, "You know all about goodness."

Her innocence made me laugh. "I'm as much a sinner as any other, and I know no more of goodness than any other."

She shook her head. "You would never hurt me."

The look on her face sobered me. "Have others hurt you, Balbina?"

She dropped her head again, refusing once more to look at me. I reached for her and lifted her chin until her eyes met mine. I saw her tears for the first time.

"If you stay with me, he won't hurt me again. He comes and lies on top of me and hurts me, but if you were here—"

I reached for her and once more pulled her close to me. "I will stay with you, Balbina. No one will hurt you that way again."

She clung to me and cried long, hard sobs that had been held prisoner inside her frail body and fragile soul for a very long time. As I held her next to me, I stroked her matted hair until she fell asleep. I considered waking her and having her walk with me back to Dominico's house. I could try to smuggle her inside, but once inside, how would I keep her hidden?

Even my own room was no sanctuary for me. Dominico, Lorenzia, and Concetta all had access to it as well as to the rest of the house, including the kitchen. I considered the little garden outside my window, but Concetta had long ago become suspicious of the time I spent there and would often come down to spy on me.

We spent the night sleeping on the ground with the dirty blanket for a pillow and our arms around each other for comfort.

I awoke just as the morning pinkened and found Balbina already awake. She was sitting up and gave me a sleepy smile when she saw me open my eyes. I sat up quickly.

"If I hurry, I can get back to Dominico's house before anyone is up," I said. "Then when they awaken, they'll think I've been there all night. I'll stay long enough to gather up breakfast and bring it back to you."

A little bit of fear clouded her eyes again. "But you will come back, won't you?"

"I'll come back," I said. "I promise."

She let me go only after I had repeated that promise at least three more times. As I hurried toward the house, the thought occurred to me that Concetta might have come to my room during the evening to help me prepare for bed. If she had come and found me not there, she would have told Dominico, or at least Lorenzia. But there was an equal chance that she had not come at all. Lately she was content to shirk her duty when she thought Dominico wouldn't know.

When I arrived at the gate that led to the courtyard of Dominico's house, I hesitated, trying to decide whether to enter by the front door or make my way around to the back. Since there was no one in sight, and since I knew Dominico would be preoccupied in his office on the first floor, if, indeed, he was there at all, I decided to save the time it would take me to go to the back and enter through the front instead.

He was waiting for me in the hallway that separated his large office from the sitting room and dining room.

I looked at him. He was angry; I could see that in the set of his jaw and in the way he snapped his riding crop in the palm of his hand. His eyes were black glass hiding something deep inside. I started to speak, although I had no idea what I would say. Before I got a word out, he grabbed my hair and pulled with a sudden hard jerk that sent fire into every inch of my head.

"Why do you do this?" he asked, then hit me in the face with the riding crop before I could answer. "Do you think I enjoy this?" he asked in a tone that made me understand that the thing hiding inside him was a strange kind of sadness. I felt something snap in my shoulder as he threw me against the wall. The pain bent me over, and I slid to the floor. I felt the sting of leather on my face again and heard his words: "Out all night with them. You've gone from whore to overly pious." When I bent over to protect my face, I felt the knotted tips of the leather crop dig into my back. "I warned you." It took only

233

a few blows to tear the thin dress I wore. "If I don't do this, others will think I'm weak." Something warm crawled down my back. "Others will think . . ."

A scarlet puddle on the floor.

I remember nothing after that until I awoke, surrounded by darkness. It took me a moment to realize I was lying on my side in my bed and that my eyes were swollen shut. One of my arms was bandaged tight across my breasts, and yellow fingers of pain clawed at my back and the tender skin around my mouth. How long had I been there? What would happen to Balbina if I didn't get back to her soon?

Chapter 16

WHEN I WAS ABLE to open my eyes enough for a tiny slit of light, I arose from my bed and retrieved Colin's letter from its secret hiding place beneath the heavy chest that held my dresses and my cloak. I pressed it close to my body, trying to absorb the words into my heart. When I heard footsteps in the hall, I hid it either under my pillow or in the folds of my skirt if I was up. That thin piece of vellum with its odd markings and hidden meaning was the only comfort I had for several days while I waited for my body to heal.

At first Concetta was the only one who came to my room. She was sullen and withdrawn and she still spoke to me only when necessary. I knew she was angry because her betrayal of me had not earned her the rewards she expected. Lorenzia seldom came to my room at all by this time. To my surprise, however, Dominico visited me several times during my two weeks of recovery.

The first time was on the third day after he beat me, and my eyes had not yet opened. I was sitting up in bed with the damp cloth on my forehead that Concetta had begrudgingly placed there as a meager defense against the fever that burned my body.

He entered and spoke my name. The sound of his voice both startled me and filled me with dread. Had I somehow managed to displease him again without knowing it? Was he here to mete out more punishment?

"Concetta tells me you fare well." His voice sounded uncommonly weak to me.

"I'm not able to open my eyes, and I burn with fever." In spite of my apprehension, there was a certain amount of anger and resentment in my voice.

"Time is a great healer, and you have always healed quickly in the past." His words, I suppose, were meant to comfort me. "Is there anything you wish?" he asked, still in his listless voice.

"I should like to go to church. As soon as I am able." I had found that, in spite of the anger and doubt I felt toward God, I missed the solace that surrounded my soul when I prayed, and I missed the sense of peace I felt in the little chapel of the Virgin. I was not yet ready to acknowledge the presence of God. I could acknowledge only my need for the comfort I found in the house dedicated to him.

Dominico's response surprised me. "Of course you may go to church. It will be good for you to confess your sins that have brought such grief to both of us." His voice became even feebler, and I sensed that he sat himself on the edge of my bed. "Your past sins with the one who got a bastard on you have made me suspicious. Surely you have the brains to see that. Whether this time you were coupling with another priest like a

236

harlot or simply helping your damnable poor and forgetting the hour like a child, I don't know. Either way, you must learn obedience. Ah, this headache!" he said. "These headaches make me wild. Make me lose patience with you. But you cause them with your disobedience. Can't you see how you twist me in circles? Ah, this ungodly affliction!"

"Send for the physician," I said, with more impatience than pity in my words.

"Physician! They're all frauds! Nothing but asses. That whore Fausta was more clever with medicines than any physician."

"Then send for her," I said, knowing full well that he would never do that.

I sensed him rise from the bed and move toward the door. "Bah!" he said. "However much I might wish for her medicine, I never want to see that whore in my house again." With that, I heard the door slam.

His stay was even briefer the next two times he visited. I attributed that, as well as the absence of his lust for me, to his continuing headache. All I could feel was gratitude. Perhaps it was uncharitable of me to be so unconcerned for his health and so focused on my own. Nevertheless, I found it difficult to feel pity for him.

Within a short time I felt well enough and could open my eyes sufficiently to venture out of the house.

"The master has bidden me go to church," I said to Concetta when I met her at the foot of the stairs on my way out. I said it loud enough for Lorenzia to hear should she be any-where other than sequestered in her bedroom, and also for Do-minico to hear, in case he'd forgotten his earlier admonition. I was in neither the mood nor the physical condition to face the consequences of his disapproval.

My first thought, once I was on the street in front of Do-minico's house, was to hasten first to the spot near the market square where I was most likely to find Balbina, but my recent beating made me cautious. If, by some chance, I was being fol-lowed, I shouldn't do anything to arouse suspicion. I went di-rectly to the church, thinking whoever might be following me would lose patience if I stayed long enough, and then I could go seek out Balbina. As soon as my eyes adjusted to the faint yellow light inside the church, I made my way to the little chapel on the left side of the long cavern.

The Virgin was there, as always, her gaze directed down-ward, a faint smile on her lips, and her arms slightly lifted, palms up—the pose that had always and even now welcomed and calmed me. I might have fallen at her feet in an attempt to reclaim my old piety, had I not noticed immediately that she was not alone. The kneeling figure in front of her was so small she might have gone unnoticed except for a slight twitching of the shoulders. It took me a moment to realize that it was a child whose shoulders heaved with sobs, and a moment longer to recognize her.

"Balbina?" I spoke only in a whisper, but it was enough to make her turn around to face me.

"Margherita!" She fell at my feet and kissed them, then used the hem of my dress to wipe the tears from her eyes. "Margherita," she said again, looking up at me. "He has hurt you again. I knew it. I knew that was the only reason that would keep you away. But I remembered your devotion to the Holy Mother, and I have prayed to her every day to bring you back to us. Now she has done it."

I reached for her with my one good arm and brought her to her feet. "You're not well, either," I said, looking at the circles under her eyes, visible even in the dim light of the church.

She shrugged. "I'm no worse than the others, and better now that I've found you again."

"I never meant to abandon you," I said. "I've not been able to leave my room until today, and I planned to go to you as soon as—"

"I know," she said. "I knew you would come. The Holy Mother told me you would."

"She told you? How—"

"And look!" she interrupted me, ignoring my question and thrusting her arm toward me, the one that had oozed with pus and putrification the last time I saw her. "Your kiss has healed it," she said. "Everyone says you are truly a saint, and now you have healed me and blessed me with your kiss."

Her words gave me an eerie feeling, as if I were somehow

being surrounded by a great whirlwind, as if I were being swept up into it and had to fight my way back to stand on the cool stone floor of the church.

"It must have been . . ." I hesitated, not knowing what to say. I had almost said that it had not been me, but God or the Blessed Mother who had healed her, but then I remembered my recent refusal to acknowledge either of them.

"Sometimes blessings come to us in the oddest ways," Balbina said, "like the time a few days ago when I was hungry. It had been so long since you had brought your basket of food I thought even God had abandoned us. Then I found, just outside the gate, a bit of bread someone dropped. I believe it was from your favorite saint—the Blessed Mother—or maybe your other saint, the one you call the Magdalene. You know, the one you said used to be a sinner herself and understands our own sinful nature?"

She went on talking in her tinkling child's voice while the statue of the Holy Mother of God smiled down upon us. I was thinking of Balbina's accidental discovery of a bit of bread when she was hungry. Was it really one of my saints who had provided it? Or was it merely a coincidence that someone had dropped a morsel? What about the time I prayed to Saint Mary of Magdala for help in escaping my garden prison and thought she hadn't heard me; then I found the discarded pieces of slate that served as stepping-stones for me? Or the prayer for a way to return to the garden when I thought the donkey was only happenstance? What about the visions of the Holy Mother when I needed her most? Why, then, had she not saved my child? Was there something I needed to learn from that tragedy? If so, why such a cruel method of teaching? I had no answers. I had only the Holy Mother's loving smile as I stood there with the one I'd come to think of as my daughter, and I had the whirlwind circling around me again.

"Margherita!" Balbina said, bringing me out of my trance. "Margherita, are you all right?"

"Yes," I said, and took her hand, leading her toward the Virgin's altar to kneel with me. We prayed together until I sensed Balbina growing restless. Or had I prayed? I'm not sure I did. All I did was close my eyes and empty my mind, trying to find God. There was no voice to let me know I'd found him. There was only a sense of peace. As I mentioned, I was never good at praying.

When Balbina and I walked out of the church and down the steps together, I was surprised to see Fausta walking toward us. As before, I recognized her once again by the dress I'd given her, which now hung even more loosely than before on her thin frame.

"Lady Margherita! At last! I've come every day for more than two weeks looking for you. I thought of going to your house, but I was afraid Dominico would . . ." She stopped speaking and stared at me, my arm bandaged tight to my chest, my swollen eyes, and bruised face. "Oh, my poor lady, the devil has been at you again, I see." Her already watery eyes brimmed over with tears, and she reached a dry and fleshless, hay-rake hand to touch me.

"It's nothing," I said, wanting to comfort her. "There are others who suffer more."

"Fausta? Is that you? Have you grown old so soon?" Balbina scrutinized her with the guilelessness of a child.

Fausta frowned at her. "It's me, all right, and call me old if you will, but you'll be a hag yourself soon enough." She hacked a phlegmy cough, spit a bloody wad on the church steps, and squinted at the girl. "And who might you be?"

"Balbina. Pippa's daughter."

"Oh, you're Pippa's whelp. I remember you." Her eyes moved from Balbina to me and back to Balbina again. "Didn't take you long to find a new tit to suck, did it? Just see that you stay clear of the old devil's whip as well as his lust, and you'll fare well." She looked at me again. "He beat you for bringing the little wench into his fine nest, did he?"

"No," I said. "For staying in her poor nest for a night."

Fausta came out with another wet laugh that filled her mouth with bloody froth. Her expression sobered as she spit it out and wiped her mouth with the back of her arm. "Don't stir his anger, lady. Not even with your goodness. He's evil."

"Sometimes I think it's his headaches that turn him toward anger, so it's not really evil but illness that makes him do as he does."

Fausta gave a derisive snort.

"He says the headaches make him wild," I added.

"Bah! He is evil even when he has no maladies." She spit the words out like phlegm.

"He mentioned a potion you used to give him to stop the headaches. Perhaps if you could tell me what it is and where you got it, I could give it to him to dull his pain, and he would spare me—"

"Me? Help the old devil out of his misery? Ha! Let him suffer in . . ." She stopped speaking and studied my face a moment. "Ah, but am I too hasty? You were about to say that if he's not ailing, perhaps his mood would be better, and he would spare the whip . . . ?" She looked at me silently for a moment longer; then her face rearranged itself, and she gave me a weak smile. "I'll bring the potion to the back door today when the church bells ring at noon. Give it to him before he sleeps, but it's best not to tell him it came from me, lest the old devil be too stubborn to accept it."

"You have the heart of a saint, Fausta, to give succor even to your enemy."

"Don't call me saint," she said, hacking the words out with one of her coughing fits. "It's you I would help, not the old devil." Once again she spit and wiped her mouth with her forearm. "Later today. When the church bells ring for noon," she said, struggling for breath as she turned to walk away. She turned back once and pointed to Balbina. "You! Whelp! Mind you do nothing to harm Lady Margherita!" She was hardly able to utter the words for lack of breath.

"Wait!" Balbina called just as Fausta turned away again. "I would go with you!"

"Ha!" Fausta gave her a dismissive wave without turning around. I could hear her wheezing until she disappeared around the corner toward the row of shabby hovels. I had to hold tight to Balbina's hand to keep her from following her.

"You won't follow her!" My voice was harsh. "You won't follow her path."

"I will!" she said, struggling with all of the strength of her frail body to free herself from me.

"Balbina, you must listen to me," I said, trying to hold on to her with one hand and arm.

Her eyes met mine, and she ceased her struggling. "Don't you see? I can't go back where I was," she said with a calm that surprised me. "I have no one to protect me now. The man . . . he comes every night and . . . and hurts me. Shames me. Fausta is one of my kind. Maybe she can—"

I pulled her close to me, overwhelmed with sadness. "Oh, Balbina, even I can't protect you. If I bring you home with me my husband will beat us both." I stroked her filthy hair and dampened it with my tears. She took advantage of the moment and ran away from me, headed the same direction Fausta had gone.

"Balbina! Balbina, wait! I . . . I'll find a way to help you. You don't have to go the way of Fausta."

She stopped and turned around, looking at me without speaking for a moment. Finally she said, "You can find a way to help?"

"Yes." There was more confidence in that word than I felt.

"How?"

"I . . . will take you to my family." I don't know where those words came from. I hadn't seen my family in over a year. I was not allowed to go to the square on market day, and I dared not risk being gone long enough for the daylong walk to and from the duke's estate, where they lived.

"You have a family?" Balbina was clearly puzzled.

"Peasants," I said. "You may have seen them on market day. They come sometimes. Especially in the autumn."

"It's too early for autumn. It's still summer." Her words made her seem determined to resist my help, but she was walking toward me, albeit with more caution than eagerness.

"Yes," I said. "They're likely working in the fields. Unless . . ."

"Unless?"

"Unless the duke bids them come. Or if there is need for something they can buy at the market."

"Today is market day," she said.

"So it is," I said, although in truth I had lost all track of it.

Balbina walked toward me, holding out her hand. "Come. Let's go to market."

*   *   *

245

It was not as I remembered it. There were fewer people and the mood was more somber, even in the section where the exotic trinkets, spices, and foods from faraway places were sold. Perhaps it was early in the season, or maybe it was because Teresa was not at my side, so full of life and making everything seem exciting. Perhaps it was simply that in the past year I had been robbed of my youth and grown old too soon.

"They should be somewhere along here," I said, leading Balbina to the section near the center where we usually set up our wares. With Balbina's hand in mine, I searched all along the pathway between booths, looking for a familiar face. Not only did I fail to find my family, I saw no one I recognized. I also kept a cautious eye on customers who roamed the pathways and stopped to bargain at the booths. It wouldn't do for anyone I knew to see me. Word would surely get back to Dominico that I had been there.

"Do you see them?" Balbina asked.

"Hush," I said, not wanting her to attract attention to us. I was beginning to be sorry that I had suggested looking for my family. I should have known better than to raise Balbina's hopes. I was about to give up and suggest we leave when I saw a face I recognized.

It was the woman known as Dolcina—Augustino's mother. The past year had not been kind to her. Her plump, round face had been replaced with a thinner, more haggard one, and the man who shared the booth with her and who was busy filling bags with what must have been last year's grain was not Jacobo, Augustino's father.

"Dolcina?" I kept my voice low and quiet as I approached her booth. "Dolcina? Is that you?"

She looked at me, scowling and without recognition at first; finally her eyes narrowed and she cocked her head. "Margherita? It's you, is it?"

"Yes," I said. "It's me, Margherita."

"Well!" She gave a little derisive laugh. "Not the plump merchant's wife I expected. Look at you! Beats you, does he? I always said you would be a stubborn one. It's best my Augustino was spared the likes of you."

"And how is Augustino?"

Her eyes hardened. "Dead. Like the rest of 'em."

My breath hung suspended somewhere in my throat. "Dead?"

"Black Death. His flesh turned as black as the bottom of my shoe. Full of sores. Vomiting blood. Just like all of them."

"Who . . . who else . . ."

"Oh, don't go thinking you're too good for it to touch yourself. Your mother, your father, the little one. They lie in their graves just like the others."

All the strings that held me together broke, and I felt myself shattering. Balbina's hand gripped my arm to keep me from sinking.

"And Teresa?" The words came out of me choked and hoarse.

Dolcina shrugged. "She was spared, but she walked away one night. Who knows where?"

"Teresa. Spared." Relief made me weak again.

"Some of us were," Dolcina said. "Some of us weren't. It's a cruel God who takes hearty men like my Augustino and my husband and spares the likes of your sister. What's a slip of a girl worth?" She waved a hand in disgust and moved toward her sacks of grain. After only a few steps she half turned toward me and spoke over her shoulder. "And don't go thinking it can't blacken and kill the high and mighty such as yourself. It will be in the town before you know it. You best make your confession and prepare your soul now."

I hardly remember Balbina leading me away from the booth. We were near the edge of the market square when she spoke to me.

"I'll go to Fausta," she said. "It's my best choice."

"They're dead," I said. "Even the baby. Where is Teresa?" I was mumbling jumbled thoughts. My response didn't make sense.

"I'll see that you get home." She took my hand.

By the time we reached Dominico's house, I'd regained enough of my senses to know I couldn't take Balbina to the front door. We walked around to the alley to the back door that opened into the kitchen.

"Good-bye, Margherita," she said just as I was about to step inside. "I'm so sorry about your family. I will pray for God to comfort you with the Holy Spirit."

"Wait!" I called to her as she turned away. "You . . . you must stay here. You can't go back."

"No," she said. "I can't stay. Your husband will beat you if I stay."

"Come inside!" Sorrow had robbed me of my patience, and my voice was harsh. I grabbed her arm and gave her a quick, hard pull, forcing her into the kitchen with me. My roughness made her stumble, and we made an untidy racket as we both entered the house.

"Who's there?" There was alarm in Rufina's voice and surprise in her eyes as she hurried toward us.

"Mistress?" She sounded even more surprised and alarmed. Because of my wounds, it had been weeks since she had seen me. I had been confined to my room, and Dominico had forbidden her to visit me this time. The sight of the street urchin I had dragged inside alarmed her even more. She knew what Dominico would do to me if he saw her.

"Mistress, have you gone insane? You can't bring her in here!" Her voice sounded improperly harsh and scolding, but I knew it was only because of her concern.

"Don't scold her," Balbina said, speaking for the first time since we'd entered. "She's had a terrible blow. The Black Death has claimed all of her family."

Rufina stared wide-eyed at the little ruffian and then at me. "The Black Death," she whispered. "I heard it was in the countryside. It will be here soon." She made the sign of the cross.

The church bells rang out, louder than usual, it seemed to me, and I was momentarily startled.

"Hide her. In the larder," I said, shoving Balbina toward Rufina. "I have an errand." I hurried toward the door. I wanted to be waiting there when Fausta arrived in order to lessen the risk of her being seen. I still had no idea of what I would do with Balbina, but she would be safe in the larder for now.

The alley was deserted as I stepped outside, just as I expected it to be. After all, the church bells had only just rung, and it would take Fausta several minutes to reach the house. However, I had waited less than a minute when I noticed a figure standing in the shadows several yards away. In spite of the gathering heat, the figure wore a long, dark cloak, and the face was covered with a hood. It looked very much like the pictures of hollow-faced Death I had seen in drawings.

It is the Black Death, I thought as it moved slowly but ever closer to me. The Black Death. Come to claim me.

It was neither the face of death nor Fausta's face that I saw when the figure came within a few feet of me and threw back the hood. It was Maria, the woman from the area of *la prostituta* who had mocked me and laughed at me when I first went there looking for Fausta, the one who had been a midwife.

"Here," she said in a hoarse whisper as she shoved a crude clay vial into my hand. "Fausta said you need this. Give him a draft now, and if he doesn't sleep, give him another tonight before his supper." She gave a quick nervous glance over her shoulder. "I wouldn't let Fausta come. She's too ill." She returned the hood to cover her face, and walked away, staying in the shadows with her head down. She knew, as well as I, that it was dangerous for her to be in this neighborhood, and even more dangerous for the two of us to be seen together.

Rufina met me with a barrage of words as I entered the kitchen again. "What were you doing out there? Who was that you were talking to? And what about that girl in the larder? We can't leave her there forever. If the master sees her, we'll all be on the street."

"I know, I know." My voice trembled, along with the hand that held the vial. "I . . . I'll think of something."

"Oh, my poor mistress," Rufina said, coming to me and kneeling at my feet. "Forgive me. You've lost your family, and I make your burden worse by scolding you. It's only that I am afraid for you. You've suffered too much."

"Stand, Rufina. There is nothing to forgive. I will find a way. God help me, I must find a way." Was that a prayer I had just uttered? Or merely an oath? I felt terribly confused. But I wasn't alone. Fausta, Rufina, Grimani, Balbina, and perhaps even Maria loved me and wanted the best for me. And my saints. Could it be they had never really left me? Were they sending all this love my way? I looked down at the vial I held in my hand.

"I must go to Dominico," I said. "I have a potion that will stop the pain in his head and allow him to sleep. While he sleeps I will pray for God to tell me what I must do."

251

If only I could believe that, I thought as I left the kitchen. Perhaps I was only pretending to have faith because I could think of nothing else to do. But I was too drained, too frightened, too filled with grief to contemplate the absence of God.

When I didn't find Dominico in his office, I knew he would be in his bedchamber, sick and in pain. I met Lorenzia on the stairs on my way up to his room.

"Where are you going?" she asked in her cruel voice.

"To Dominico. I would take him a potion for his head."

"Leave him alone! Haven't you done him enough harm?" She tried to grab the vial I held, but I managed to keep it from her and to escape her reach. I hurried away, leaving her fuming on the stairs.

I knocked softly at Dominico's door, and when he didn't answer I opened it slowly and peeked into the darkened room. He lay upon his bed, his arm across his eyes. A sea foam of crumpled bedcoverings surrounded him, along with the familiar sour-milk scent of himself.

"Who's there?" His voice, though weakened by pain, still held an edge of cruelty.

"I've brought you a potion. For your headache."

"Get out! I'll have none of it!"

"It's Fausta's remedy."

He lifted his arm from across his eyes and raised his head enough to look at me. I could tell that the movement caused him pain.

"Where did you get it?" His voice was a low growl.

"I asked her for it when I saw her near the church. She sent it—"

"You converse with whores? I was right all along. You're nothing but a whore yourself!"

His anger made me tremble and think I had made a mistake by telling the truth. But if I'd told him I'd gotten the potion from someone else, he would refuse it, saying that if it weren't Fausta's remedy it wouldn't work.

He let his head fall back to the pillow and brought his arm up to cover his eyes again, too sick with pain to attack me. "You! You are the cause of all of my misery. And of your own as well. Why do you not behave as I wish? Why? Why? Don't you know I love you? That in spite of everything, I love you?"

It was the first time he'd ever declared his love for me, and it stunned me. I didn't know what I should do except to obey him, to leave as he had commanded me. I was almost to the door when he called out to me.

"Wait!"

I turned around. His arm was still over his eyes.

"You did that for me? Asked that woman for the remedy?"

"Yes, my husband."

"Are you certain it's Fausta's remedy?"

"I am certain."

He waited a moment, then motioned with his free hand

for me to approach him. "Leave it there. On the table." His eyes were still covered.

I placed the vial on the table next to his bed and walked as noiselessly as possible out of the room.

Concetta was the first to know he was dead. She found him cold and bloodless when she brought him his supper. The physician who was summoned said he had died of an apoplexy.

Fausta came to visit later that evening. She was almost too weak to walk, but she didn't go around the alley to the back door; she entered boldly through the front door and told Concetta she wished to see me. Her only words, which she spoke through a spasm of coughing before she turned away and disappeared down the street, were, "We have our ways. We take care of our own."

Epilogue

AND SO ENDS the account of Margherita of San Severino, known by those who loved her as Margherita the Barefooted. By the grace of God and through my love for her, I, Sister Anne Maria of the order of Saint Benedict, who was formerly known as Balbina Òrfana, undertook the task of writing down her words as she spake them shortly before her death when she was in her seventieth year.

I now near the end of my own life here in the Convent of Saint Elizabeth in the March of Ancona, where my love for Margherita has never ceased, and, indeed, has grown stronger in the same manner that my love for Our Lord has grown. So strong was my love for her that when I took the veil and vowed fidelity as the bride of Christ, I felt unworthy to take her name when I was asked to choose one as a symbol of leaving the world for my life as a servant. I chose instead to take the name of our dear Margherita's saints, who were, as she has so faithfully recorded, Maria, *Madre de Dios*, and Saint Maria de Magdala, and to take the name of the mother of the Blessed Mother as well, in memory of Margherita's lost motherhood.

Having grown old in the service of Our Lord and awaiting

my time to enter into the presence of divine intelligence, I feel compelled to complete with my own poor words the story of Margherita the Barefooted. May God forgive me for waiting so long.

Had she been called even one day later to join Our Father in heavenly bliss, I know that she would have finished her tale by reporting that Fausta, whom she loved as Christ loves sinners, died only a few days after Dominico Vasari quit this earth and was called to answer for his life before the throne of God. Fausta, growing weaker by the hour because of the ravages of the consumption, succumbed to death alone in the hovel Margherita has so aptly described. It was Margherita who found her when she went to ask her to live with her in the great house that had been Dominico Vasari's.

Margherita didn't know that the house would not be hers. It and the business went to Dominico's only surviving family member, Signora Lorenzia. As was the custom in our part of the Holy Roman Empire, Margherita was given a part of the estate for her maintenance. It provided only a meager living for her, but she continued to share what she had with the poor. Lorenzia never ceased to protest the sum provided for Margherita until the day of her death in the year of Our Lord 1347, one year before the Black Death struck all of Italy with such great force. Greed and avarice such as Lorenzia's are deadlier than the plague because they consume the soul as well as the body, eating at both until they are mere shells surrounding nothing.

Rufina and Grimani continued to live in the house with Lorenzia and later with Margherita when she returned after Lorenzia's death. It is a wonder, if not a miracle, that Margherita was able to reclaim the estate, since, as we all know, widows have no standing and their wealth is usually confiscated by greedy rulers. However, she was so loved by most of the town that no one dared try to take what was rightfully hers. However, when she gained possession of the house, the cradle Father Colin had made was gone. Perhaps Lorenzia burned it as firewood.

Grimani and Rufina were loved by Margherita as if they were mother and father, which, indeed, they had become and, of course, stayed on with her. Concetta stayed on as well, there being no other place for her. She professed devotion to Margherita, as was her wont, but I am certain she never loved her. As for Teresa, although Margherita searched her entire life for her sister, she never found her.

She continued, yea even intensified, her work and her mercies with the poor of San Severino with such love and generosity that before her death the entire city called her blessed and saint. It now remains only for the Holy Father and his noble princes to confirm her sainthood, which, by the grace of God, will not be long in coming. Margherita never ceased humbling herself before the poor by appearing to them barefoot and in rags. Her wealth was apparent only in her generosity.

I, though unworthy of even her smile, was blessed with her

generosity no less than others. I lived with her as her daughter for a time until she divined, without my having to tell her, my desire to enter into the vows of chastity in the service of Our Lord. Such was the purity, grace, and power of her spirit. Not having means of my own to enter into that life because of my poverty, the blessed Margherita paid my dowry to the convent and visited me regularly throughout my novitiate and beyond.

Through her generosity by sending me here, I learned the art of letters. It was my selfish desire to learn so that I might read all the books in the world and thus acquire all of the knowledge of the world. May God forgive me for that prideful sin.

It seemed to me later that I might redeem myself by undertaking to write down Margherita's story as she related it to me. May my poor and unworthy efforts serve to glorify her.

And now, having transcribed her words and this, my unworthy addition, there remains but one more task for me to fulfill before I am taken from this earth, and that is to translate the letter of Colin to Margherita. At first I thought the letter lost, since Margherita never asked me to translate it for her. I would never have intruded upon her privacy by asking her for it, and I didn't discover it until several years after her death. It was, as she had said years before, beneath a chest that belonged to her and which was transported to me at the convent. By some miracle the abbess allowed me to keep it in my cell, perhaps because she, too, had heard of the piety of Margherita the Barefooted.

In my ignorance, I had not considered that Margherita's reference to the letter being "beneath the chest" could have implied the presence of a false bottom. By the grace of God, I discovered the apparatus one day and the letter inside.

May my aged hand remain steady as I translate the letter here.

To Margherita, beloved by Christ, servant and handmaiden to Him who is greatest above all. I, Colin, His unworthy servant, greet you.

Knowing full well that it is God's will that we both continue our service to Him and that I must never, to my sorrow, see you again except in heaven, where we both will be purified and made worthy of His presence, I send you this epistle. I abide now in a cell far away from you in the monastery of San Pietro to which I have come out of obedience. I saw your sorrow when I departed and trust that mine was equally apparent. As you no doubt know, it is our privilege to suffer for Him who suffered and died for us, and thus it is, I believe, that God set our paths to cross and to taste, however innocently and briefly, the bitter fruits of forbidden love.

You, beloved of God, have suffered much for Him that makes your presence all the more sweet to Him as well as to me. I am not worthy to stand in your shadow, sinner that I am, and though I am still sorely tempted to show my love to you in the ways of the flesh, I know that I must not. It is not the salvation of my own soul I consider when I keep myself from you. It is my fear that I will distract you from your mission. God has a great need for your work.

I must remain in the monastery of San Pietro, where I pray daily for you and for your protection against the great torment that has become your lot through your husband. I pray also for myself to put aside my lust so that we both may serve the Creator.

If lust depart from me one day, love will not. You will always be my beloved. I cannot forget the beauty of your face, your lovely eyes, or your most sensuous mouth. As great as your worldly beauty may be, it is your soul that is most beautiful, and which I love with all of my heart and, I confess, all of my flesh. I cannot even pray for forgiveness for desiring you. I can only hope that, were it not for God's greater design, He could look upon our love and call it good.

I beseech you, my sister in Christ and, yea, my beloved in the flesh, to continue in the service of Him who has died for our sins knowing that you are loved not only by Him, but that you are loved by another as well, one who is willing to perish in the fires of hell rather than denounce his love for you.

Live, and fare you well. Pray for me, for I love you too much.